Had someone been inside her cottage? And if so, why?

Eric had not bothered to turn on the light. He pointed to the desk in the corner near the sliding glass doors, and she noticed the drawer ajar in the darkened room. A few of her notes were scattered on the floor, the various files she'd collected from the private investigator shuffled through as if someone had searched them.

Her pulse clamored. Someone *had* been there. But why would they be interested in her files?

Eric's hand gently touched hers. "Someone was in here."

She jerked her head up. "I know."

"Do you have any idea why?"

Because they know why you're in Savannah, she realized. *And they don't want you to learn the truth....*

Dear Harlequin Intrigue Reader,

We've got an intoxicating lineup crackling with passion and peril that's guaranteed to lure you to Harlequin Intrigue this month!

Danger and desire abound in *As Darkness Fell*—the first of two installments in Joanna Wayne's HIDDEN PASSIONS: Full Moon Madness companion series. In this stark, seductive tale, a rugged detective will go to extreme lengths to safeguard a feisty reporter who is the object of a killer's obsession. Then temptation and terror go hand in hand in *Lone Rider Bodyguard* when Harper Allen launches her brand-new miniseries, MEN OF THE DOUBLE B RANCH.

Will revenge give way to sweet salvation in *Undercover Avenger* by Rita Herron? Find out in the ongoing NIGHTHAWK ISLAND series. If you're searching high and low for a thrilling romantic suspense tale that will also satisfy your craving for adventure— you'll be positively riveted by *Bounty Hunter Ransom* from Kara Lennox's CODE OF THE COBRA.

Just when you thought it was safe to sleep with the lights off…*Guardian of her Heart* by Linda O. Johnston— the latest offering in our BACHELORS AT LARGE promotion—will send shivers down your spine. And don't let down your guard quite yet. Lisa Childs caps off a month of spine-tingling suspense with a gripping thriller about a madman bent on revenge in *Bridal Reconnaissance*. You won't want to miss this unforgettable debut of our new DEAD BOLT promotion.

Here's hoping these smoldering Harlequin Intrigue novels will inspire some romantic dreams of your own this Valentine's Day!

Enjoy,

Denise O'Sullivan
Senior Editor
Harlequin Intrigue

UNDERCOVER AVENGER
RITA HERRON

TORONTO • NEW YORK • LONDON
AMSTERDAM • PARIS • SYDNEY • HAMBURG
STOCKHOLM • ATHENS • TOKYO • MILAN • MADRID
PRAGUE • WARSAW • BUDAPEST • AUCKLAND

ISBN 0-373-22755-8

UNDERCOVER AVENGER

Copyright © 2004 by Rita B. Herron

This edition published by arrangement with Harlequin Books S.A.

® and TM are trademarks of the publisher. Trademarks indicated with ® are registered in the United States Patent and Trademark Office, the Canadian Trade Marks Office and in other countries.

Visit us at www.eHarlequin.com

Printed in U.S.A.

ABOUT THE AUTHOR

Award-winning author Rita Herron wrote her first book when she was twelve, but didn't think real people grew up to be writers. Now she writes so she doesn't have to get a *real* job. A former kindergarten teacher and workshop leader, she traded her storytelling for kids for writing romantic comedies and romantic suspense. She lives in Georgia with her own romance hero and three kids. She loves to hear from readers, so please write her at P.O. Box 921225, Norcross, GA 30092-1225, or visit her Web site at www.ritaherron.com.

Books by Rita Herron

†Nighthawk Island
*The Hartwell Hope Chests

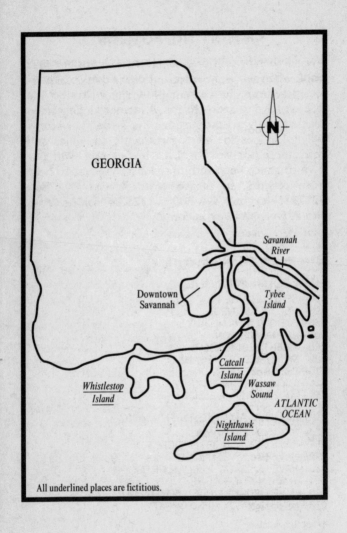

GEORGIA

Savannah
River

Downtown
Savannah

Tybee
Island

Catcall
Island

Wassaw
Sound

Whistlestop
Island

ATLANTIC
OCEAN

Nighthawk
Island

N

All underlined places are fictitious.

CAST OF CHARACTERS

Eric Caldwell—A scarred man in search of revenge.

Melissa Fagan—She was abandoned as a child and is on a dangerous quest to find her identity.

Luke Devlin—Eric's FBI contact. Does he know something about CIRP that he's hiding?

Ian Hall—The new director of CIRP. Is he whom he claims to be?

Arnold Hughes—The former director of CIRP who is wanted by the police. Has he resurfaced from the dead with a new face?

Candace Latone—Is this psychotic woman really Melissa's mother?

Robert Latone—This powerful foreign diplomat will kill anyone who threatens his power and his name.

Edward Moor—Latone's right-hand man and confidant.

Dennis Hopkins—A scientist dabbling with brainwashing techniques.

Wallace Thacker—A chemist who has recently transferred to CIRP. Could he be Hughes?

Helen Anderson—The elderly nurse has been at the research hospital for years. Does she have secrets that might help Melissa find her birth parents?

Walter Stinson—One of Melissa's patients. Did he really lose his leg to diabetes?

Louise Philigreen—A confused woman who lost a baby years ago.

To Melissa Endlich for all your support!

And to the Georgia Romance Writers
for being the greatest chapter ever!
Thanks a bunch for turning out at the signings.

Prologue

Eric Caldwell walked a fine line with the law, but he didn't care. He had trusted the Feds before and people had died. He didn't intend to let it happen to this witness.

Even if he and his brother, Cain, fought again. Cain, always the good guy, the one on the right side of the law. The man who never saw the grays.

The only color Eric did see.

"Come on, Eric, where's the witness in the Bronsky case?" Cain asked.

"What?" Sarcasm laced Eric's voice. "Did the police lose another witness?"

"We do the best we can," his brother said. "Do you know where he is?"

Eric grabbed a Marlboro and pushed it into the corner of his mouth. "Sorry, can't help you, bro."

Cain hissed, his message ringing loud and clear. Eric was lying, but Cain knew better than to push it. Eric would do whatever he could to keep the witness alive. "You can't go around undermining the cops and the FBI, Eric, or killing every criminal who escapes the system."

He glared at Cain over the duffel bag he'd been packing. "I didn't kill anyone."

Cain's gaze turned deadly. "I don't want to see your vigilante ways get you in trouble. It's like you're on a death mission, taking everything into your own hands." Cain's voice thickened. "One day you're going to cross the wrong people."

Eric ignored the concern in Cain's warning, zipped his bag, then threw it over his shoulder, grabbed his keys and strode toward the door. "Like you don't cross the wrong kind all the time."

"It's not the same thing," Cain argued. "I have people covering me. You're on your own."

Eric hesitated. "You could quit the force and help me. Make it your New Year's resolution."

"New Year's has come and gone," Cain said. Their gazes locked briefly and Eric's stomach clenched. His brother was serious. "Join the force, Eric, and work with the law, not against us."

But Eric could not fit the mold. "I guess we hit that impasse again." He snagged his laptop off the counter.

Cain's jaw tightened. "Watch your back. If you get into trouble—"

"Then you'll be there to help me." A cocky grin slid onto Eric's face. "Now, I'd love to stay and talk politics but I gotta go."

Cain caught his arm before he could fly past. "Where are you going?"

Eric stared him down hard, the way he had when they were boys and they'd argued over whether or not to interfere when things had gone sour at home. When their father had taken his rage out on their mother and them. "I have business to finish," he said between clenched teeth. "Legitimate business at the ranch."

His brother studied him, didn't believe him. Eric didn't care.

Or maybe he did, but he would do what he had to do anyway.

Mottled storm clouds rolled across the sky as he headed outside, thunder rumbling above the trees. The wind howled off the lake, a haunting reminder of the bleakness that had become his life.

He didn't have time for self-analysis, though. He had to get the witness to a safe house, then meet that woman his friend Polenta had sent his way. She'd sounded desperate, as if she was in trouble. And there was a kid involved. Some baby named Simon. The woman hadn't made sense. She claimed they were after the baby, that he was the product of a research experiment.

He'd known then he had to help her and the child. He'd even considered confiding in Cain, but she had turned to him for a reason. Because she couldn't trust the cops.

The reason he did what he did.

Eric could never say no to a woman or child in trouble. Not when his own past haunted him, when memories of his mother's suicide still sent sweat trickling down his spine. Years ago, he'd started working with an underground organization to help women escape abusive homes so they didn't meet the same fate, and their children didn't suffer from abuse themselves. Someone had to help them break the cycle.

He jogged down the front-porch steps two at a time,

heading toward the lean-to where he'd parked the Jeep. Thankfully, his brother followed him to the porch. The witness was hiding in the back room, waiting to escape out the side door, then slip through the woods to the SUV.

Rocks and gravel sprayed beneath his boots as he walked, the sting of his brother's disapproval burning his back. He shrugged it off, tossed his duffel bag into the back seat along with his computer and saw the witness crawl into the passenger seat. He waited until Cain turned before he went to retrieve the cash he kept stashed in the shed for emergencies.

Shaded by the thick forest of trees between his property and the road, he stepped toward the knotty pines. But a sudden explosion rent the air, the impact throwing him against a tree. Glass shards and flying metal assaulted him. He banged his head and tasted dirt, then jerked around on his knees in shock. His Jeep had exploded. A fireball rolled off it toward the sky. Ignoring the blinding pain that seared him, he lurched forward to rescue the witness, but another explosion rocked the ground and sent him hurling backward again into the woods.

Fire breathed against his skin, catching his clothes and singeing his arms and legs. A jagged rock pierced his skull.

The world went momentarily dark, the crackle of fire eating into the night. Eric pulled himself from the haze and tried to yell for help, but his vocal cords shut down. The smoke and fire robbed him of air. He coughed, inhaling the acrid odor of his own burning flesh. Pain, intense and raw, seared him. Flames clawed at his face, and pieces of hot metal stabbed his thigh. Then dizziness swept over him.

He released a silent scream into the night, welcoming death and telling his brother goodbye.

Chapter One

Three Months Later

"Did you find my birth parents?" Melissa Fagan asked.

Larry Dormer, a local Atlanta private investigator she'd hired, hesitated before answering. "I hit a lot of dead ends."

He was stalling. Melissa steadied her voice to hide the disappointment. She wanted a name, just a name. At least for starters. "So, why did you call me in, Mr. Dormer?"

"You told me to let you know if I found anything. I have a lead." Anxiety emanated from him in the uneven breaths that rasped through the air, along with the scent of his perspiration. He'd cracked his knuckles more than once, as well, reaching for cigarettes, then fighting the urge, a definite sign of nerves.

Instead, he drummed a pencil on his desk. How bad could it be? Had he located her parents and been told they didn't want to be found? Were they shady people?

"You know most records are sealed—"

"Just tell me," she said, growing impatient. She could feel his pity, hear the disapproval in his voice, sense he was holding back. He didn't think she should search for people who might not want to be found. She should respect their privacy. She'd heard it all before. But she had to know the truth. "Look, I understand how difficult it is to hack into confidential files. Believe me, I've tried several sources. But I want to know everything you learned."

"You're sure? You registered in the national database for adopted children, so if your parents were looking for you, they'd be able to contact you."

"Maybe they're not certain I'd welcome them."

He still hesitated. "All right. But you may not like what you discover."

"I'm well aware of that." All those years of foster care, she'd prayed she'd be adopted. Or that her mother or father would suddenly appear and rescue her from a life of being shuffled from one place to another. That hadn't happened.

Now at twenty-six, she had no such illusions that her life would be so idyllic.

Her mother had left her on the doorstep of a church with no note, nothing except a tiny handmade crocheted bonnet with a pink ribbon. She had no idea why she'd been deserted. If she did, maybe she could overcome this dreadful sense of abandonment.

Besides, it would be nice to feel connected to someone else in the world. Not to feel so alone. To at least know the truth about the woman who'd given birth to her.

He still hesitated, studying her over square glasses, giving her time to contemplate her options.

What if her mother or father had searched for her but had encountered the same brick walls she had? Or what if her parents had given her away because they couldn't handle parenting an imperfect child?

She massaged her temple, fighting an agitation-induced headache. The one that indicated the on-slaught of a seizure. Her medication helped immensely, but occasionally she still experienced the episodes. They were mild, not epileptic in nature, and her symptoms mimicked a bad migraine—she became disoriented, slipped into a trancelike state for a few minutes—but they still embarrassed her and made her feel flawed. Besides, the attacks always left her phys-ically exhausted and slightly depressed.

Other questions assailed her. What if her mother had never told her father about her existence? What if one of her parents could accept her and be proud that she'd become an independent young woman? A physical therapist, when so many people hadn't believed she'd succeed.

What if your parents are happily married to other people and have families of their own? What if they're ashamed of you, the bastard child?

What if you weren't born out of a night of passion? Are you prepared for an ugly truth like that?

How could she go on not knowing, though? She'd lived in darkness all her life, her past an empty vac-uum—at least this was one door she could open, look through, then close it if need be.

She braced herself for the worst. "Tell me what you discovered."

He sighed and reached for a cigarette, this time relenting and lighting up. The stench of smoke filled the air, his shaky rasp of contentment following. "Your mother's name was Candace Latone."

Candace? She savored the name for a moment. "Was Latone her maiden name or married name?"

"She wasn't married."

"What else can you tell me?"

"She was young. Gave birth to you in Savannah, Georgia." He hesitated, his reluctancy to answer her palpable.

"What?" Anger tightened her throat. "I'm paying you for the truth, not to sugarcoat it."

"All right." He wheezed, his cheap suit coat rattling as he swiped at the perspiration on his face. "She spent some time in a hospital down there."

"You mean she worked at one? Was she a nurse, an aide, a doctor? What?"

"She was a patient, Miss Fagan. She attended college in Savannah and got involved in some kind of research experiment at the hospital where she volunteered."

"What kind of experiment?"

"I haven't been able to find that out. Records are sealed. No one is talking."

"And my father?"

"Nothing so far."

Her mind veered off on a tangent—could the research experiment have caused her seizure disorder? The doctors hadn't been able to explain the exact cause, but suggested it was genetic. And though not life threatening, the disorder deterred people from adopting her. Worse, she was afraid she might pass it on to a child. Maybe if she discovered the cause, the doctors could prevent her offspring from inheriting the condition.

"If I were you, I'd forget the search." He stood, inhaling smoke and shuffling papers, his demeanor indicating an end to their meeting.

"Can you keep looking?" Melissa asked.

"I told you everything, Miss Fagan. Now, I'd let sleeping dogs lie."

Melissa shivered and gripped the chair edge. She didn't believe him. He was hiding something.

Still, learning her mother's name should have been enough. Melissa had been born in Savannah; she had a place to start. But the fact that Candace had been involved in a research project, and that Melissa suffered from seizures no one could explain, triggered more questions. "All right, thank you for your help."

He snapped the file closed as if glad to be finished with it. "Goodbye, Miss Fagan."

Melissa headed to the door, still contemplating his odd behavior. The elevator dinged, and she waited for the people to exit, then stepped inside, fighting off the stench of body odors, stifling perfumes and smoke lingering inside.

Frustration clawed at her as the doors closed, claustrophobia choking her. She pulled at her collar and inhaled, wrestling with bitter memories of being locked in a small room by her foster parents. They'd claimed they wanted to prevent her from wandering around at night, had been afraid she'd stumble into something. Instead, they'd confined her like a prisoner.

The elevator whirled to a stop, the doors buzzed open, and she stepped outside, breathing in the fresh air. A warm spring breeze brushed her neck, the scents of freshly baked bread and Italian cuisine floating from the neighborhood restaurant. The hum of Atlanta traffic whizzed around her—a horn blowing, a siren wailing, pedestrians passing. A homeless man in ratty clothes reeking of booze and filth hugged a bottle of wine to his chest, his glassy eyes staring up at her, glazed and disoriented. Compassion filled her. She understood how it felt to be homeless, unwanted.

She slipped inside a neighboring bagel shop, bought a bagful of bagels and a cup of hot coffee, then hurried out and handed them to him. Then she hailed a cab. At least she had more information than she'd had the day before.

Tomorrow, she would check out the research park in Savannah and get a job there. Once she located her parents, she could put the past to rest.

ERIC STILL COULDN'T believe he was alive.

Although the pain he had endured for the past few months had been excruciating, the doctors had claimed his strong will had brought him through.

Eric knew differently. He had survived so he could get revenge.

So he could find the person responsible for killing his witness and make him pay. And when he'd learned that the killer had also tried to murder his brother, an innocent woman and baby, he'd decided to do whatever was necessary to catch him.

Even work with the FBI.

"You can't go undercover, Eric. For God's sake, you're in a wheelchair. You're too vulnerable."

Eric rubbed a hand along his jaw, ignoring the distress on Cain's face. "I don't want your damn pity, Cain. And I won't be in this chair long."

Still uncomfortable with the chair and his new image, Eric gripped the metal arms. But his new face beat the hideous one he'd awakened to three months before. And he would walk again, no matter how much physical therapy he had to endure.

"Hell, Cain, I thought you'd be glad I finally hooked up with the Feds."

"But working undercover at the Coastal Island Research Park is too risky," Cain argued. "What if someone realizes who you are?"

Eric pointed to the hospital mirror. "Look at me, bro. You didn't even recognize me. How will anyone at CIRP, when they've never seen me?" He wheeled the chair toward the door. "I'm the last person they'd expect to show up as a patient."

"I don't like that, either," Cain said. "Damn. If it weren't for Alanna and Simon, I'd take the job."

"No, they need you," Eric said. "Besides, the people at CIRP would recognize you."

His brother couldn't argue with that point. "If Hughes has resurfaced, and they discover you're with the Feds, there's no telling what they'll do to you. Do you have any idea the lengths some of those scientists have resorted to in order to cover themselves?"

His brother was right. The Feds had already briefed him on earlier questionable events at the center.

Eric's mind ticked back to what he knew so far. Arnold Hughes had co-founded the research park, but years ago, he'd tried to sell research to a foreign source, then committed murder to cover his actions. When the police tried to arrest him, he'd escaped. His boat had exploded, but his body had never been found. Recent rumors suggested he'd resurfaced. That he'd not only supported a memory transplant experiment in which a former Savannah cop, Clayton Fox, had had his memory erased and been made to believe he was a man named Cole Turner, but he'd spearheaded an experiment to explore creating the perfect child. The child had been Simon—the baby his brother's wife had protected by kidnapping him from the center.

Hughes was Simon's father, only he didn't know it.

And now a manhunt was on for Hughes.

The fact that the Feds suspected Hughes had resurfaced with a new identity had sparked the idea for Eric to capitalize on his own new face and work undercover. Ironic, but cunning—he'd use their own game to trap them. He'd even adopted a fake last name, Collier, to cover himself.

"The doctors are going to patch up my body," Eric said with a wry grin. "It's the least they can do after destroying it."

"That's just it, you're not physically strong enough to defend yourself right now."

Cain's comment cut to the bone. "Another reason I'm having therapy. Besides, I need time to heal before the doctors can perform more skin grafts. I might as well be useful in the meantime."' The rehab arrangement at CIRP offered private bungalows on-site for recovery, which would allow him mobility and a beach view, a helluva lot better setup than another god-awful hospital, or having to arrange transportation from his own cabin to a rehab facility on a daily basis. He refused to be dependent on his brother.

Cain caught his arm just as Eric reached for the doorknob. Déjà vu flooded him. Another time when his brother had tried to stop him. If he'd listened to him then, the witness might still be alive.

But one look at the wheelchair, and he had to follow through. After all, it was spring. Cain had a new wife and a baby. A life to live.

Eric's future was bleak. No spring roses or kids or lovers in his future. He had nothing but a battered, scarred body. And a dark soul, to boot.

One no woman would want.

All he had to live for was his revenge.

A WEEK LATER, MELISSA had landed a job at the Coastal Island Research Park Hospital, and moved into one of the small cottages on Skidaway Island CIRP had built for employees. But she'd hit a brick wall in Savannah when she tried to locate Candace Latone. Apparently, there weren't any Latones living in the area, either that or they weren't listed in the phone book. It was possible her mother had come to Savannah as a student from another city. Although Melissa's funds were limited, her investigative skills were even more so. She would have to hire another P.I. to search for Candace.

.Unless she discovered information at the school or hospital that would lead her to her mother.

People were funny about keeping secrets, even ones over twenty years old. She had to pursue her search slowly, so as not to upset the tide should someone object to her jimmying the closed doors of their lives. Last year, she'd read an article about an adopted child who'd been murdered because she'd unearthed the truth about her parentage. Her father had been a well-known politician who'd wanted to cover his mistakes.

Mistake—was that what she had been?

Shaking off the troubling reminder that she'd been unwanted, she considered the possibilities. But she doubted she'd discover anything quite so newsworthy or dramatic in her past. Still, Dormer's warning had unnerved her, as had the stories she'd heard about the research park since she'd arrived—unethical research experiments, the death of the former director, the disappearance of another, Arnold Hughes, the murder attempt on a scientist and his wife when they had defied the institute. All too scary.

Deciding to lie low the first few days, make friends, acquaint herself with the patient load and staff, she focused on meeting the nurses, doctors and other therapists. She had just finished with her first patient, a child who'd suffered two broken legs in a car accident, when Nancy, one of the college-age girls who volunteered at the center, nudged her. Melissa's gaze veered toward the door, where a broad-shouldered man with dark brown hair rolled toward them in a wheelchair. Masculinity and sex appeal oozed from him, along with the anguish evident in his tightly set jaw and black expression. He hated the wheelchair, that was obvious. Hated his weakness, that was obvious, too.

She didn't blame him. She hated her own weaknesses.

"Not bad for an old guy," Nancy murmured.

Melissa winced. He was only thirty-four. His name, Eric Collier. His chart revealed he was over six feet tall, weighed two hundred pounds. He didn't have to stand up for her to see that his body was muscular. His face was nice looking, too, a broad jaw, angular with a firm nose and deep-set dark eyes.

"What's his story?" Nancy asked.

Melissa explained his injuries. "He also suffered burns over twenty-five percent of his body, he's had some skin grafts, waiting for more."

Nancy shivered. "What happened?"

"Some kind of car accident. Apparently there was a gas leak and his car exploded."

Nancy backed away, stricken. "Poor man. He was probably even better-looking before."

He's gorgeous anyway, Melissa wanted to say, but she didn't. She had to remain professional. She never got involved with patients. And she wouldn't make an exception here.

But the injuries and scars didn't faze her as they did the young girl beside her. The courage the patients possessed did—everyone she worked with had a story. Dreams lost, shattered bodies and bruised self-esteem. Some gave in to pity, others fought hard not to succumb to the depression. To regain those dreams and their lives. With every failure and setback, she felt their frustration. With every success, their joy. And for those who tried to give up, she rallied harder to encourage them to fight back.

This one looked like a fighter.

The wheelchair rolled to a stop, the man's hard gaze pinning her as he looked up into her eyes. His were a muddy brown, almost black. Angry. Full of pride. Challenge. Pain.

"Eric Cal... Collier," he said. "I'm here for my session."

She extended her hand, ignoring the fact that he was as handsome as sin. Anger radiated from his every pore in palpable waves, an attitude of aloofness surrounding him that would have been off-putting had she not seen it before. This man was not only scarred on the outside but on the inside, as well. Old wounds hadn't healed, had festered instead, maybe all the way to his soul. She understood about those kinds of wounds too. She'd lived with them all her life. "Melissa Fagan."

His mouth twitched as if he was trying for a smile but couldn't force his lips to form one. She smiled for him instead. She'd seen tough men before and understood their difficulty in accepting help, as well as their own imperfections.

Especially when they had to depend on a woman.

Male pride and all that. This guy possessed it in spades.

"We'll start over here, Mr. Collier." She directed him to a desk in the corner for their first consultation. As soon as she sat, he relaxed slightly, although for a fleeting second his gaze skittered over her in an almost

appreciative way, as if he'd noticed her as a man no-
tices a woman. Good, some part of him wasn't dead.

She'd wondered at first.

As a therapist, in the past, a few patients had been
attracted to her. At first. But once they started the sessions, they usually wound up hating her. Hating her
for pushing them. For punishing their bodies. For reminding them she could walk without help and they
couldn't.

She didn't let their attitudes affect her, either. In the
end, when they stood and walked out on their own
two feet, free of their crutches, tolerating their temper
outbursts was worth it.

Thankfully, putting herself more on his level helped
dissipate some of his tension. She'd seen that reaction
before, too. Men despised women towering over them.
Control issues.

"Well," she said, inflecting a cheerfulness in her
voice she used with her patients. "It looks like we
have our work cut out for us, Mr. Collier." She reviewed his injuries and described the strategy for getting him back in shape, outlining basic exercise routines to be performed at the center and at home.
"Remember, it takes time to regain your strength. You
have to be patient."

His curt nod warned her not to count on it.

She gestured toward the workout area. "Are you
ready to get out of that chair, Eric?"

He seemed momentarily startled she'd used his first
name, but he dismissed it quickly, then nodded, somber but determined.

"Good, but remember, you'll have to take it one

step at a time, one day at a time.'' She smiled, hoping to temper her comment. ''If you overdo, you can damage yourself further and cause a setback, so remember when I tell you to stop, it's for a reason.''

''Right.'' His sarcastic reply wasn't lost on her. She'd have to stay on top of him or he'd ignore caution.

She pointed to the locker room and watched him wheel toward it, his broad shoulders stiff, his head held high. She hoped he would maintain the attitude.

He would need it to survive the long grueling sessions ahead of him.

ERIC STEELED HIMSELF against the instant attraction he felt for Melissa Fagan while he changed into workout shorts and a T-shirt. He should have worn them to the session, but pride had made him stall in revealing his scars. Especially when he'd heard his therapist was going to be female.

Disgust filled him for even momentarily noticing her beauty. This woman had read his chart. She knew the extent of his injuries. She would have to help him stand, help him learn to walk again.

She would have to touch his ugly marred flesh.

He could not think of her as a woman.

Still, he sucked in a sharp breath at the thought of exposing himself to her, though after all he'd endured in the hospital the last three months, he should be accustomed to it. The baths, the skin grafts, the constant poking and prodding. But somehow revealing his wounds to Melissa made him feel even more naked and raw.

Focus on the job. On catching Hughes.

His resolve set, he wheeled through the doors to the locker room, but the young blond candy striper winced as her gaze landed on his scarred thigh. He gritted his teeth and rolled past her, stopping directly in front of Melissa Fagan, daring her to do the same. She didn't. She simply offered him a smile and gestured for him to follow as if his injuries didn't faze her.

He gave her credit for not flinching, when he had almost gagged the first time the doctor had removed the bandages and he'd seen the mounds of discolored, purplish-red mangled flesh that had once been his solid, slick muscular thighs and arms and chest.

Of course, she was simply doing a job. Maybe she'd become immune to reacting to patients the way he'd forced himself to be impersonal when he dealt with victims. God knows, he'd seen some horrors in the past few years.

He remembered the courage the brutalized women he'd helped had shown as he gritted his teeth and endured the painful stretching and warm-up exercises she instructed him to do. He wouldn't complain. Wouldn't growl at her or curse even though he desperately needed to vent.

He would suffer through torture if it would make him whole again.

Damn it, his thigh completely cramped. The shooting pain radiated all the way from his upper leg down through his calf. Nausea gripped his stomach from the impact of the muscle spasm, but he sucked in air to control it.

"That's right, breathe in, out." Melissa gently kneaded the muscle, slowly stretching his leg and fitting his foot against her thigh. He focused on the deep-breathing exercises to stifle the rage of temper that attacked him at his helplessness.

Her silky hair swayed around her shoulders as she leaned forward to press her fingers into his leg, rubbing and massaging with long nimble strokes that felt like heaven.

He stared at her hands. He'd never quite appreciated the power of the pleasure they could offer a man. At least, not when the act wasn't sexual. Her fingers pressed harder as she leaned forward to continue her ministrations, and he glimpsed the perfect pale skin of her neck. But he didn't dwell on it or allow himself to enjoy the sweet fragrance of her soap and shampoo or the way her lips were the color of sun-ripened raspberries. And when images of her long dark hair cascading across his stomach intervened, he banished them, as well.

"That's the reason we start with those basic warm-up and stretching exercises," she said softly. "Although cramps are inevitable, especially in the early stages of therapy." She angled her face toward him and smiled. The light softened her already pale green eyes. "Feeling better?"

He nodded, reminding himself that her smile and the soft words she murmured in that thick, sultry voice were intended to encourage him to work harder. They were also filled with compassion that he didn't want to need or feel.

Because feeling only meant more pain. And he had reached his limit.

THE SIGHT OF ERIC'S proud stubborn chin thrust high as he wheeled toward the locker room stirred Melissa's admiration even more, but the sensations she'd felt when she'd massaged the cramps in his legs had her heart pounding. When she'd helped him into the whirlpool, she had watched the bubbling water ooze over his flesh and had ached to soothe the tension from his strained face, the strain caused by working so hard to camouflage his agony.

She had never reacted this way to a patient before.

Touching and massaging body parts had become rote, impersonal. Yet, her stomach had fluttered when she'd placed Eric's foot against her leg and touched his thigh. He had struggled to contain his reaction, although she'd glimpsed the fine sheen of perspiration that had beaded his lip when her fingers had pressed against his sensitive skin.

Hating herself for allowing personal feelings to intervene during work, she justified her reaction as a product of loneliness. She'd moved to a new place. She felt isolated and wanted to connect with someone.

She had been lonely and isolated her entire life.

Dismissing the melancholy thought, she wiped the back of her neck with a gym towel and hurried toward the break room for coffee. She could not start lusting after her patients. Good grief, she would lose her job. Not that she planned to stay here long. No, as soon as she discovered her parents' identity and location, she'd hightail it to wherever they lived.

Eric Collier's tortured dark eyes rose to taunt her.

The sooner she left town, the better.

Deciding to forgo the coffee, she went to search for the old records. They would either be kept on microfiche or stored in the basement of the main facility, not in the rehab building, so she detoured through the breezeway that connected the rehab building to the main hospital. Confidential or not, she had to see if the hospital still had records on Candace Latone.

She checked over her shoulder as she hurried down the hallway to the restricted area, determined to keep a low profile so as not to arouse suspicion.

EVERY MUSCLE AND JOINT in Eric's body throbbed with pain. Even his teeth hurt.

It still hadn't kept him from noticing Melissa Fagan though, or reacting as a man would to a woman's touch.

Damn. He tossed the towel into the dirty-clothes bin and wheeled toward the exit. Forget the shower. He'd take one when he returned to his room. Where he had privacy and strangers didn't have to watch him drag his butt from the chair to another one to wash his battered body.

He hesitated, chastising himself for indulging in a pity party. He had noticed others suffering while they worked through their own therapy. A young boy, about twelve. What was his story? An elderly woman—did she have family? A tiny toddler with leg braces—God.

Seeing them had affected him. At least enough to jolt him out of his own depression and finish the reps Melissa had assigned him. She'd warned him not to overdo.

Hell, he'd barely been able to manage the exercises she'd asked of him.

He hated the weakness. Hated immobility. Hated that a beautiful woman like Melissa had to see his ugliness.

He'd told Cain he could do his job, but what if he couldn't?

Fighting the uncertainty over his recovery, he thrust himself forward, pushing down the hall. Maybe he'd take a scenic tour of the hospital on the way out and study the layout. At least then he could say he'd started investigating. If anyone stopped him, he could always claim he'd gotten lost.

Play up the invalid bit.

Just as he rounded the corner near the bottom floor, he spotted Melissa. He wheeled to an abrupt stop, watching her from a distance. Breathing in her beauty and telling himself not to.

But a frown pulled at his mouth. She was checking over her shoulder as if she thought someone might be following her. He edged into the corner of the doorway behind the open doors so she wouldn't see him. She bit down on her lip as her gaze scanned the hall. Apparently deciding it was clear, she ducked into the doors and disappeared.

He inched the chair from behind the doorway and wheeled closer. The sign on the door said Restricted.

From the nervous look on her face, she wasn't supposed to be entering the area. So what exactly was she up to?

Chapter Two

Melissa eased down the long corridor, listening for voices or footsteps, peering at the frosted glass of the doors labeled to identify the areas. Several labs caught her attention, along with a hallway that led to another restricted area and a dark cavern of testing areas connected by steel slab doors that required special clearance and were designed with passkey codes. The entire wing felt alien and cold, the air stale. The absence of antiseptic odors or other chemical scents seemed odd in itself. Gray linoleum, light gray walls, reinforced-steel beams supported the forbidden structure. She felt as if she'd stepped into a tomb.

What exactly was going on behind those closed doors?

The sound of distant footsteps echoed from the neighboring wing, and she hesitated, planting herself in the corner as they passed. She held her breath while they crossed the opening, perspiration dotting her palms. Finally, when the footsteps faded into the distance, she veered to the right, bypassed a room marked X-rays, then spotted the file room. Wiping her damp hands on her slacks, she reached for the doorknob.

"Excuse me, what are you doing here?"

Melissa froze, possible excuses racing through her head. Taking a calming breath, she turned and forced a smile. "I'm new to the center and need to review some patient files."

"Your name?"

A security guard faced her, clad in a gray uniform, a name tag attached to the stiff pocket of his shirt. His posture indicated he meant business, his tone implied she was in trouble.

"Melissa Fagan. I'm a physical therapist working with the rehabilitation program."

He copied down her name, then checked it against a master list from his clipboard. His finger thumped onto the line where she must have been listed, because his gaze rose to meet hers. Still skeptical. "Do you have clearance to be in this area?"

Melissa played dumb. "Clearance?"

His puffy lips twitched in irritation. "Yes, this is a restricted area."

Melissa glanced around, pretending innocence. "Actually, it's only my first day here. I must have missed the sign and didn't realize."

"Any files you need for patients are housed in the computer system in the rehab area. Older ones are also kept in the basement of that area."

"Oh, I see." She offered him a watery smile. "I guess I got confused. But thanks for straightening that out. I've always been directionally impaired."

His eyes narrowed as if he thought she was lying

or virtually incompetent. "I'll have to report you were in the area."

She turned to escape, but his gruff voice added, "CIRP is very careful of its restricted areas, so don't let it happen again, Miss Fagan. Snooping into confidential files and restricted areas could be dangerous."

A chill skittered up her spine. Had he meant the comment as a warning or a threat?

ERIC HAD WHEELED HIS CHAIR to a corner and was studying the doors where Melissa had disappeared, wondering how difficult it would be to break CIRP's security codes. He wished like hell he could walk so he could delve into the case rather than speculate.

The doors suddenly opened and Melissa reappeared. Her green eyes flickered with panic as she stepped into the light, and her hands were trembling. Although earlier he'd sensed steely determination in the woman when she'd pushed him through his therapy, vulnerability shadowed her pale face now.

What was she up to?

Determined not to be caught watching her, he spun the chair around and wheeled to the nearest exit. Barreling down the handicap ramp, he cursed again when the chair caught in a piece of loose gravel and jolted forward. It took him a second to dislodge the stone before he could continue. He followed the concrete path to the bungalows, grateful CIRP had designed the facility to give patients as much mobility as possible. Being robbed of his independence hacked at his self-esteem, but it would be intolerable if he had to rely on his brother to drive him back and forth to a rehab facility, or if he was confined to a hospital room like the other facilities Cain had mentioned.

Another reason CIRP had appealed to him.

That and finding Hughes and getting revenge for the death of the witness his people had killed. This afternoon he'd review the list of employees, including every scientist at CIRP and the CEO who'd replaced Hughes and start trying to pinpoint which man might be Hughes in disguise.

Fishing the key from his pocket, he unlocked the door to the cabin, tossed his duffel bag inside, then rolled across the slick wood floor, his mind ticking back to Melissa Fagan. Why had she been snooping around in the restricted area? What was she looking for?

Could she possibly be an undercover detective posing as a physical therapist? If not, what other explanation could there be?

But if she was an undercover cop or agent, why hadn't he been informed?

A testament to his lack of faith and truth—one minute he'd been attracted to her, the next he suspected her of subterfuge.

Only one way to find out. The shower beckoned, but first he grabbed his cell phone and called his contact at the FBI, Luke Devlin a forty-something workaholic with a badass attitude. Eric normally despised the slick-suited agents, but he had connected with Devlin immediately. Something dark and edgy tainted the man's gray eyes, a haunted look Eric knew was mirrored in his own.

"Devlin here. What's up?"

"It's Eric. Is there another agent working at CIRP undercover?"

Devlin hesitated. "Why do you ask?"

Eric frowned. Devlin had a habit of answering a question with a question. "Would you tell me if someone else was working with you? If you guys are undermining me or working another angle, I need to know."

"Don't get so defensive. I simply wanted to know if you'd seen something suspicious. I assume you did or you wouldn't be asking."

Eric bottled his temper, and explained about Melissa Fagan's odd behavior.

"No, she's not one of ours. That doesn't mean she's not working for someone else though."

"The locals maybe?"

"Actually, we're coordinating with them, so no," Devlin said, "but I'll check her out and call you back."

"Thanks. I'll keep an eye on her. If she's not a cop or agent, maybe she's connected to Hughes's return," Eric suggested. "Or who knows, she might be here to steal research of some kind."

"Right, keep an eye on her." Devlin sighed. "Anything else to report?"

"Nothing yet. I…just had my first session today."

"It's going to take time to heal," Devlin said. "Be patient."

Eric ignored the comment. "I'll review the data you sent and see if I can narrow down the list of suspects fitting Hughes's profile." Eric agreed to report in a few days, then hung up, looked down at his battered body and tried to lift his leg. It weighed a ton and refused to move as he wanted. Damn it.

Be patient.

Easy for a mobile man to say, not so easy when you couldn't take a baby step. Instead of the shower, he dragged himself up on the bed and collapsed, unable to fight the lingering fatigue from his accident.

But even in his sleep, he couldn't rest.

He dreamed about the explosion. The witness he'd been protecting clawed at the inside of the car, screaming for help. His eyes were glassy with pain and horror. Blood gushed down his face.

Eric lay helpless on the ground, blazing metal trapping him. His body was on fire, burning, burning, burning.

MELISSA WAS STILL A WRECK when she returned to the rehab center for her next patient session. How would she ever bypass security and locate those files when CIRP had the entire place under lock and key?

She definitely hadn't started out well by getting caught and receiving a warning on her first day of the job.

Shaking off the anxiety that she might never find the answers she wanted, she pasted on a smile and focused on her patients. The first, a teenager who'd been in an alcohol-related accident and barely survived. Thankfully, he had been humbled by the experience. The second, a war veteran who'd lost a leg from diabetes. He'd been fitted with a prosthesis but had not handled the adjustment very well. The last was a salt-and-pepper-haired doctor in his early fifties who'd been injured in the terrorist attacks on 9/11.

When she finished charting the patient records for the day, she slipped into the employee lounge. Helen Anderson, one of the nurses she'd met when she arrived, waved her over. In her late fifties, she had a mop of curly brown hair dusted in gray. Padded with a few extra pounds, but not heavy, she mothered the other staff members.

"Sit down and put your feet up, honey. You've had a busy morning."

Melissa nodded, dumped a packet of sweetener in her coffee and plopped onto the love seat across from the woman. "How long have you worked here, Helen?"

Helen popped a powdered doughnut hole into her mouth, then dabbed at the corners. "Seems like forever," she said with a laugh. "But it's only been thirty years."

Since before Melissa was born. Maybe this woman did know something....

"I imagine the center's changed a lot."

"Changed and grown. When the hospital was first built, it was very small, everything was housed in one building. Now it's all spread out, and the research facilities have expanded. Whew, I can't keep up."

"I know, I've read about some of the cutting-edge techniques." Melissa had studied the layout. The psychiatric ward was actually in another building, which was attached by crosswalks, as were the rehab facility and the main hospital. Other buildings housed experimental-research centers and laboratories scattered across Catcall Island, with additional ones on the more remote Whistlestop and Nighthawk Islands.

Helen shook her head. "Hopefully, all the trouble's passed."

"But you're worried?"

"You hear things, you know, about questionable projects out on Nighthawk Island. Did you know they named the island after some mysterious nighthawk who preys on people, not just other animals?"

"No, but that's interesting." Melissa sipped her coffee. "They conduct government experiments on the island?"

"Yes, but everything's so danged secretive. One of the founders, Arnold Hughes, actually killed a scientist a long time ago because Hughes wanted to sell the man's research to a higher bidder. And when this cop named Clayton Fox started nosing around last year, they replaced his memory with another man's." She shuddered. "And then there was that poor baby…"

Melissa chewed her lip. So the things she'd read on-line had been true.

Helen twisted her hands. "Maybe I'm getting paranoid in my old age, but I worry they're doing chemical and biological warfare research," she admitted, her agitation growing. "With all this talk of terrorist attacks and war, it could be awful. And what if they release chemicals or germs on the people through the water?"

"It is scary. Since 9/11, I've had a few nightmares myself."

Helen rubbed her fingers together while Melissa struggled for a way to ask more questions without arousing suspicion. "Have you always worked with rehab patients, or did you ever work in other departments?"

"I moved around when I first came here, trying to find my place." Helen folded her arms across her plump belly. "Worked in labor and delivery awhile, the cardiac unit, the E.R., then I got my PT license."

"Delivering babies must have been exciting."

Helen shrugged, then stiffened and stood, dumping her coffee into the trash. An odd expression streaked her face. Panic? "I... Break's over. I have to get back to work now."

Without another word, she hurried from the room, looking agitated and eager to escape more questions.

Melissa frowned. What had triggered her reaction?

Two HOURS LATER, Eric finally dragged himself from bed to the shower. Even with the handicap rails, pulling his body from the chair into the tub and onto the customized seat took enormous effort and taxed his upper-body strength. The grueling morning session had taken its toll. Although he was tempted to add a few reps to the series of stretching exercises Melissa Fagan had assigned him, he worried he'd barely complete the basic ones.

At any rate, he wasn't supposed to tackle them until after dinner. Maybe he'd take a nice long stroll outside—in his chair—for some fresh air, scope out the facility.

Maybe he'd even run into his therapist. Not that he wanted to see her again...

'And even if you did, he thought, what would she want with some scarred, crippled man?

Disgusted with himself, he toweled off, dressed in baggy sweats and a T-shirt, then wheeled outside to get some air. He couldn't let himself become obsessed with things he couldn't have. Like a woman.

But there she was.

Standing off the path, looking out at the ocean. A stiff wind flung her hair around her face. Her cheeks looked softer in the fading sunlight, but her eyes looked troubled. What exactly was her story? And why did he care if she was lonely? He wasn't anyone's hero, not anymore…

Unable to resist the forces drawing him to her, though, he wheeled over to her. The creak of his chair alerted her to his presence and she glanced his way. A small smile lifted the corner of her mouth.

"Hi, Eric."

God, he loved the way she murmured his name. He must be desperate. "Hi."

"How are you feeling tonight?"

He shrugged. "I hate to admit it, but you wore me out earlier."

A twinkle replaced the sadness in her eyes, and he grinned.

"It's always hard at first," she said softly. "It'll get easier."

But never quite back to normal. He knew it. But he didn't want to believe it.

"You like the ocean?" he asked.

She nodded and angled her face into the wind again, once again melancholy. "I haven't spent much time at the beach, though. The sea is so vast, it looks like it could go on forever.''

There was that sadness in her voice again. ''I know what you mean.'' Damn. He was bad at chit chat. Didn't know how to talk to a woman anymore. ''Back home I have a cabin on the lake. At night, I like to sit outside, look at the stars and the moon. It's peaceful.''

She tucked a strand of hair behind her ear and glanced down at him. Moonlight played off her hair, making him itch to touch it. Her lips parted, eliciting fantasies of long slow kisses that went on forever, just like the ocean.

But he couldn't even reach her, much less kiss her. Not sitting down.

A reminder of his condition.

Reality crashed over him, just like the waves breaking on the shore. ''I guess I'd better go. Can I walk you to your cottage?'' The minute the words came out, he realized how ridiculous they sounded.

But she didn't react. Probably out of pity.

''Sure.'' He wheeled beside her, the tension crackling as they crossed the path. When they reached her cottage, she turned to him. ''Thanks, Eric. I'll see you tomorrow.''

''Yeah.''

''Get some rest.''

Any illusion he might have harbored about her seeing him as a man was shattered. She saw him as a patient.

And he'd damn well better remember it.

Furious with himself, he wheeled back to his cabin. He'd do his job, learn to walk again and get the hell

out of Savannah. Determined, he spread out the computer printout listing all the CIRP employees. He studied ages and basic body sizes, narrowing the field
down to five potential men who might be Hughes. The
new CEO of CIRP was a definite possibility. But
claiming Hughes's original position would almost be
too obvious. Another possibility was Dennis Hopkins,
a scientist who'd recently transferred to CIRP from the
Oakland facility in Tennessee, and a chemist, Wallace
Thacker. Of course, the list might not be complete.
With the classified projects on Nighthawk Island,
CIRP might also have employees who weren't listed
in the database the FBI had tapped into. Previously,
the police had uncovered research on experiments to
create a superhuman child and memory transplants.

What kind of projects were under way now?

"ALL RIGHT, DO WE HAVE the team put together?"

"Yes." Dennis Hopkins shuffled through the latest
data from his research study. "I'm ready to move
ahead. Preliminary results of the drugs we're testing
combined with hypnosis look good."

"Great. I have clearance to see the results."

"I'm grateful the government is being so coopera-
tive." In fact, Hopkins had been amazed when the
special agent had contacted him with a request for the
type of research work he had already begun. Brainwashing techniques had always been used by secret
government agencies, but most relied on torture. A
smile lifted his lips.

His methods were definitely more advanced, civi-
lized, ingenious.

''Are you kidding? With terrorism and the situation in the Middle East, we need your techniques yesterday.''

Pride puffed up Hopkins's chest, along with sarcasm in his response. ''I'm glad to do whatever I can for my country.''

''Right.'' The special agent on the other end of the line didn't find him amusing. ''Let me know if you have any problems, and we'll take care of them.''

Hopkins chuckled. He understood the agent's implications. Problems, as in someone snooping around. Hell, if he discovered trouble, if anyone interfered, he'd simply turn the unwanted party into a live subject for his experiment.

And he wouldn't fail as they had with the memory transplant they'd performed on that cop Clayton Fox. No, his study of the brain exceeded their original piece of work.

And he had secret government clearance to do whatever was necessary to perfect it.

Now, all he needed was the human subjects. Willing or unwilling, it really didn't matter....

Chapter Three

Two weeks later, Eric woke from another haunting nightmare of the explosion, his breathing erratic, his body drenched in sweat. The incessant itching from his scars was driving him crazy. Early morning sunlight flowed through the blinds, streaking the discolored flesh on his chest. He muttered an oath and forced himself to look at the puckered skin anyway. To see himself the way he knew others did, a man branded by his disfigurement, a cicatrix, like a rock standing alone on the side of a mountain.

Half an hour later, he faced Melissa. She seemed tired, too, and distracted, as if she hadn't slept well either. But since that night by the ocean, he'd staunchly avoided any personal conversation.

Her perfect mouth parted in a smile. "Ready to get started?"

Damn. He wanted to kiss her. He grunted instead, adopting his detached persona as the heat from her fingertips began to massage the ache in his calf.

The other part of him that ached would have to continue to do so.

The past two weeks had been a series of mindless, torturous exercises and grueling physical routines that had stolen the last vestiges of his pride and reminded him that he hadn't just lost skin and mobility in the accident, but endurance as well.

But he would walk again. He couldn't quit, or he'd never exact his revenge.

Admittedly, seeing Melissa Fagan's encouraging smile eased the pain.

She finished the warm-up exercises, then coached him through stretches. There were times during the sessions when he hated her. Times she pushed him to the limits. Times she forced him to continue when he wanted to succumb to the mind numbing pity and self-recrimination that snuck from the dark hiding places of his soul barking that he was a failure. That he should have died instead of that witness.

But in the black emptiness of his cabin at night, when the ceiling fan swirled lazily above him and he remembered the scent of Melissa's silky hair, he closed his eyes and ached to feel alive. To hold her.

He jerked upright, pulling away from her. "I can take it from here."

Her fingers paused on his upper thigh, and he gritted his teeth. "Are you sure?"

"Yes. I'm ready for the weights."

She nodded, her troubled gaze meeting his. But he had snapped at her enough over the last few days that she didn't argue. She simply offered him that damn sweet smile and gestured toward another patient.

"I'll be right over there if you need me."

He gave a clipped nod. Hell, he did need her. But not in the way she meant.

Only he'd never be able to have her.

BY THE TIME Eric got back to his cabin, he was exhausted. He had to finish this job so he could get out of Savannah. Away from Melissa.

He pulled out his notes and reviewed them. So far, he'd met each of the men he suspected to be Hughes and photographed them with the FBI's miniature camera, but he was still no closer to the truth than before. He'd heard hints of some secretive projects under way involving germ warfare, but he'd yet to access any specific information. Maybe the Feds had chosen the wrong guy for the job.

The phone rang. He stifled irritation as he swung his stiff body sideways to a sitting position to answer it. "Caldwell here."

"Eric, it's Luke Devlin."

"Yeah?"

"I discovered some interesting things about the woman you asked me to investigate."

Melissa? "Yeah?"

"Background is shady. She was an orphan, abandoned and left on the doorsteps of a church when she was a baby."

Eric's throat tightened. "Was she adopted?"

"No. Her file was dog-eared with a medical problem, some odd disorder, but the doctors couldn't pinpoint the cause. Must have scared people away."

Medical problem? Melissa Fagan appeared completely healthy, normal…no more, than normal. She had to be physically strong to perform her job.

"So, what happened to her?"

"Same old, same old. Apparently, she was juggled from one foster home to another, ended up in a group home outside Atlanta as a teen. Earned a scholarship and a degree, then attended PT school at Emory."

Impressive. But those foster homes—although the system tried, Eric had witnessed horror stories of failed results and homes that never should have been recommended for the foster care program, children battered and abused and traumatized from the results of misplacements. What was Melissa's story?

"What's she doing here at CIRP?"

Devlin's breath wheezed over the line, and Eric realized he was smoking. His hand automatically dropped to his bedside table, a self-deprecating chuckle following. He'd quit, not by choice, but during his hospital stay, he hadn't been able to smoke. The first time he'd smelled a cigarette afterwards, it had triggered memories of the scent of his own flesh burning.

"Miss Fagan recently hired a private investigator. Apparently she's trying to locate her birth parents."

"She believes they're here?"

"She was born in Savannah not long after the hospital was opened. In fact, shortly after Hughes came on board."

Eric sat up straighter, his anxiety level rising a notch. Too coincidental. The research experiments with baby Simon hadn't been the first, he was certain. One of the locals, Detective Black's sister Denise Harley, had researched methods to enhance cognitive growth, but she'd supposedly scratched the research, afraid it would fall into the wrong hands. Had the facility conducted questionable experiments back in the eighties? And if so, could Melissa be somehow connected?

No, he was jumping to conclusions, letting his imagination run away from him because of Simon. Hundreds of babies were born each year, abandoned, adopted, all normal deliveries.

Still, as he hung up, worry assaulted him. Even if there weren't any strange circumstances surrounding her birth, what would happen if she started asking questions?

Did her parents want to be found or would they rather their secrets be buried forever?

AFTER HER MORNING sessions, Melissa had tried to hack into the computer system again, but failed. Helen walked by the cafeteria and barely spared her a glance. So much for forging a friendship here. Melissa had definitely upset the woman that day when she'd asked about the labor and delivery wing. Helen had avoided her since.

Dreading her afternoon session with Eric, she finished her bagel, a slight headache pinching. To avoid a seizure, she seriously needed to destress, but how could she relax when questions from her past haunted her? Who was she? How sick had her mother been? Why hadn't one of the other family members possessed the ability to love her? What kind of people were the Latones?

They'd deserted a baby…

Unfortunately, she wouldn't find the answers in the cafeteria, so she took a pain reliever and hurried back to the rehab wing. She'd been pushing Eric hard, and he'd made great strides.

But as he entered, she recognized anger and mounting despair in his eyes. He wasn't recovering as quickly as he wanted. And although he kept his emotions sealed in a steel vault, they had been bottled so long she sensed the door might blow open any minute.

When that happened—and she knew it would, because every patient experienced the boiling point—she would be there to push him further. She refused to let him give up. Even if he did hate her. And lately, it appeared that way. His behavior might not have hurt so much if she hadn't sensed heat between them that night he'd met her by the ocean. And when he'd escorted her back to her room, she'd thought he might kiss her.

But she couldn't allow herself to get involved, especially when she needed to focus on finding out the truth about her identity.

Besides, she had never trusted enough to allow anyone close before. Not after all the times she'd been rejected. The memory of her college boyfriend's reaction to her seizure had been burned into her brain as deeply as the physical scars on Eric's body.

A body that, in spite of its scars was taut and muscular and undeniably attractive.

Her cheeks flared with heat at the thought of being intimate with him. He would be the first...only he didn't seem to want her.

He rolled toward her, and she inhaled deeply to stymie her natural reaction. Fatigue shadowed his dark eyes, the remnants of lack of sleep evident in the tiny lines around his mouth.

She wondered what he'd look like if he actually smiled.

But she doubted she'd see it anytime soon.

"Afternoon, Eric."

He simply scowled, offering no more conversation than usual.

"Have a good break?"

"Yeah, I guess."

She dragged her gaze from his face to his chart. She'd added a few more exercises to the original regimen.

He parked the chair beside the exercise equipment and flattened his hands on his thighs, beginning the sequence of warm-up exercises that had become routine for both of them. He stretched and flexed while she massaged the cramped muscle in his lower calf. His right leg seemed stronger daily, but the left one had sustained more damage and was progressing slower.

His skin felt hot to the touch, the dark hairs on his leg brushing sensitive nerve endings as she stroked and applied pressure to the muscle. He gritted his teeth, his tight jaw masking any reaction to the pain.

"How are you sleeping?" she asked as she extended his left leg and nodded for him to push against her hand.

"Fine."

"Your eyes tell a different story."

He jerked his head up, a haunted hollow look his only reply.

"The doctor could give you something so you can rest. To help with the nightmares."

"Who said I have nightmares?"

She smiled, continuing her workout as she spoke. "You wouldn't be human if you didn't, not after what you've been through."

He gripped the chair edge. "I'm sure they'll fade with time."

"Probably." She gestured toward the bars. "But talking about them might help."

"So you're offering shrink services, too?"

Melissa hesitated, sensing his coiled emotions on the verge of exploding. "I'm not a shrink, just a friend."

"Friend?" A bitter-sounding laugh rumbled from his chest. "Well, honey, I've been short on those lately."

This time her head jerked up. It was the first time he'd called her anything but Miss Fagan.

As if he decided he'd made a huge faux pas, his mouth flattened into a tight line again, and he grabbed the bar to hoist himself up. Melissa reached out an arm to help him, but he pushed her hand away.

WHAT THE HELL made him say a fool thing like that to his therapist? One minute she was suggesting he needed a shrink, the next minute he'd all but flirted with her. Eric Caldwell didn't know how to flirt anymore, or do anything but work.

Melissa Fagan felt sorry for him, nothing more.

How could she feel anything else when she saw his ugly body and touched his mangled flesh on a daily basis? When she of all people knew his limitations, that he was no longer a whole man?

As if to cement his feelings, the young candy striper watched from the corner, her gaze full of pity. Bitterness swelled inside him as he struggled to straighten his legs and put weight on them. He had to brace himself with his arms, the force causing his muscles to strain. Shoving any ideas of chitchat from his head, he ordered himself to focus. To concentrate on making his legs work the way they once had.

Until his body had forgotten.

They spent the next half hour in grueling silence, going through several reps of leg extensions and flexing exercises. Eric was tired of the tidbits of progress. He wanted to walk.

"You were in a hospital in Atlanta before this?" Melissa asked.

"Yes."

"What brought you all the way to Savannah for therapy? Atlanta has some great facilities."

"Yes, but the on-site living and ocean here appealed to me. Being confined to a hospital room was too suffocating."

Melissa smiled. "I understand the feeling. I get claustrophobic myself." She gestured for him to stop. "I think we can call it quits for today."

Eric glared at her. "No, not yet."

Melissa's gaze met his. "Remember my warning about not overdoing, Eric."

"I'm tired of this crap," Eric growled. "I want to do more. I *can* do more."

"No."

Anger fed him as he attempted to move his foot forward, but his leg refused to budge. Steeling his rage, he stared down at the appendage, willing it to move.

"Eric, you're exhausted, let's rest."

"No, damn it. I'm going to walk." Channeling every ounce of misery into determination, he pushed his foot a fraction of an inch, but his leg cramped and his knees buckled. He tried to catch himself before he went down, but his arms were shaking from the exertion, and he wound up landing on his butt, heaving for air. "Damn it, damn it, damn it." He scraped his hands through his hair, then grabbed his leg and rubbed the knotted muscle.

Melissa knelt, her soft hand on his back, angering him more. "Come on, you need to rest."

"Leave me alone." All his pent-up frustration snapped, exploding in jerky movements. He felt like a failure.

Melissa eased around in front of him, cradled his calf between her hands and kneaded the muscle, applying pressure at the pinpoints of pain and smoothing them away. She had magic hands. He felt weak, relieved, indebted.

Out of the corner of his eye, he noticed the young candy striper's sympathetic look again. Still, he was helpless to refuse Melissa's ministrations. Worse, he despised himself for not wanting her to stop, for having to accept the role of victim when he had always been the one to lend help to the weaker.

"I might as well give up." He dropped his head

forward, unable to believe he'd finally voiced his doubts.

Melissa's hands stilled. Her voice was quiet when she spoke, reassuring. "You will walk again, Eric, but you have to be patient."

"Patient?"

"Yes, you can't quit."

"Why not? It's been two weeks, and I still can't slide my foot a damn inch."

She gripped his hands in hers. "You are making progress, Eric. You can't expect damaged muscles to work without proper rest and retraining. Recovery is hard and slow, but time does heal things."

"How would you know?" His past with his family, the explosion, the cases with the women he'd worked with, all converged, blotting out any hope from the darkness. He felt as if he'd been thrown into a pit of endless gray and couldn't climb out. Ever.

She dropped her hands. "You're not the first patient I've worked with, nor will you be the last."

"That's right. I'm just a patient to you, nothing more." He fisted his hands. "You feel sorry for me—"

"I don't feel sorry for you, Eric. You've covered that yourself."

He knotted his fists. Her words hit home. Still, he was helpless to react, because all those lonely mornings of waking and wanting more from her than therapy flashed into his mind. God, he yearned to have her hands all over him, massaging more than his legs...

"I also know what it's like to overcome a physical

problem," Melissa said so quietly he almost didn't hear her.

He flattened his hands in an effort to push himself up. He remembered the report from Devlin, but he couldn't believe she had medical issues. She was too beautiful, too tough, too compassionate and strong. Her condition must have been so minor, she'd overcome it long ago. "How can you possibly understand?"

"Because I have a seizure disorder," she said matter-of-factly.

His gaze met hers. For a brief second, he realized the pain in her confession.

"I'm not epileptic," Melissa said. "But occasionally I have mild seizures. I take medication for them daily." Her voice dropped to a thready whisper. "My condition has complicated my life."

Luke had mentioned that she'd been shuffled from one home to another, never been adopted. Eric had spent his entire life helping women in need, yet now he was taking his frustrations out on her.

Good God. He was no better than his father.

Shame replaced his anger. "I'm sorry. I..."

"Now you're feeling sorry for me." Her quick flash of temper was real. Eric had no idea how to rectify his blunder. He'd just insulted her by doing the very thing he'd accused her of, offering her pity.

"Now, let's get you off the floor."

He started to apologize, but her dark look warned him to drop the subject. He gripped her arm and allowed her to help him stand.

"You want to try again?"

He nodded, more determined than ever.

The next few minutes, he forgot the darkness in his soul and his need for revenge as she murmured words of encouragement. Instead, he imagined stepping toward her, taking her in his arms and kissing those luscious pink lips. Finally, he managed to slide his foot forward a fraction of an inch.

"You did it!"

He glanced down and a ghost of a smile flitted on his mouth. Although the step had been minute, it gave him hope.

And he vowed not to unleash his rage on Melissa again.

EMOTIONS PING-PONGED in Melissa's chest as she finished her snack, the memory of Eric's first step still exhilarating her. He would progress much faster now—that one step would fuel his drive and confidence.

It was time she made progress with her own quest. She wrapped the crumbs of her snack in a paper towel and dabbed at her mouth. Nancy had hurried through her coffee to meet her boyfriend. Helen remained quiet, thumbing through a magazine. Two of the younger doctors breezed in for coffee. A third, a bone specialist, Steve Crayton, smiled at her.

"You're doing an excellent job, Miss Fagan. We're glad to have you on board."

"Thanks."

Although some of the other nurses found him attractive, something about his intense demeanor prickled at her nerves. Granted he was handsome, and well established for a man in his forties, but his eyes seemed too probing.

"I have surgery in a few minutes. I'll probably refer this patient to you afterward."

"Fine, let me know when you're ready for a consultation."

Hoping Helen would linger for a few minutes, Melissa hurried back to the center's office and slid up to the computer. Within seconds, she'd tapped into the main list of patient files, but couldn't gain access to the older records in the labor/delivery unit without a password. Hmm. She hated to be sneaky, but she had to have answers, so she searched through the drawer and found Helen's organizer. Helen had consulted it before, seemingly embarrassed that her memory sometimes failed her. She'd admitted she kept everything written down. Melissa scrolled down the list, located the woman's password and logged on. Several minutes later, she'd entered Candace Latone's name, along with the date of her own birth and had almost accessed the file, when a voice sounded behind her.

"What are you doing?"

Melissa froze. Helen's tone sounded cold. Suspicious.

Melissa scrambled for a lie, but decided to opt for the truth. She turned to her with imploring eyes. "I'm trying to find my birth parents," she said. "I know my mother's name. Maybe you remember her."

Helen's eyes darted around the room. "I can't remember every patient from years ago. And you have no right to sneak into my things. I should report you."

Melissa gave her a beseeching look. "Please don't,

Helen. I wasn't trying to hurt anyone, just locate information on my mother. I have reason to believe a woman named Candace Latone gave birth to me here, and that she gave me up for adoption.''

The woman's face blanched. ''Candace Latone?''

''Yes. Apparently she was involved in some kind of research experiment.'' Melissa wondered exactly what type of experiment. ''You knew her, didn't you?''

''I…'' Helen's hand flew to her cheek, where she picked at a loose strand of hair. ''I vaguely remember the name.''

''What happened to her?'' Melissa clutched Helen's hand. Had the scientist done something to hurt her? ''Please tell me, I have to know.''

''She wasn't quite right, you know…refused to leave Savannah.'' Her voice quavered. ''I believe her family set her up in some kind of cabin nearby.''

''Oh my gosh, you mean she's in Savannah? But I searched and didn't find any Latones.''

''Her phone number may be unlisted. The last thing I heard she lived on the Isle of Hope.''

''Do you know the address?'' Melissa asked.

''No.''

''Do you have any idea what kind of experiment she was involved in?''

''No. I wasn't aware she'd participated in anything like that.'' She fidgeted with her hands. ''Rumor said she did drugs, that's what caused her mental instability.''

Melissa frowned, then glanced up and noticed

Nancy watching them. How much had she overheard? Nancy waved. "Your next patient is here, Melissa."

"Thanks, I'll be right there."

Helen closed the files, the conversation over. But excitement filled Melissa as she worked through the afternoon sessions. The minute she finished, she climbed in her car and drove toward the Isle of Hope. The name somehow fit the moment.

What would Candace Latone think when she showed up at her door, claiming to be her daughter?

AFTER HIS AFTERNOON SESSION Eric had collapsed and dreamed about kissing Melissa. Long slow lazy kisses that had ended with them naked in his bed. Only he wasn't a scarred man, but the old Eric Caldwell, the confident man who protected others.

The dream still haunted him while he met with the plastic surgeon. Although he'd set up the consultation to discuss his own injuries, he had a secret agenda. Somehow, he had to gain access to the doctor's computer and locate files on Hughes. If he could verify that Hughes had resurfaced and locate a file with information regarding his new identity, catching him would be easier.

Dr. Crane greeted him with a handshake. "Nice to meet you, Mr. Collier. I've already reviewed your charts."

Eric nodded while Crane took a seat behind his massive desk. Eric's file was open, before-and-after photographs of his injured body spread out. Eric swallowed hard, reminding himself he looked better now than he had. At least the Atlanta doctors had repaired his face. They'd yet to complete skin grafts on his chest and left leg, though.

"You look like you're healing nicely."

Eric chuckled. "There's nothing nice about this body now."

The doctor ran long fingers through his thinning white hair. "It takes time."

"So everyone keeps telling me."

Crane nodded. "Are you satisfied with the face now, or do you want more changes?" He stood and examined Eric, probing around his cheekbones and eyes, then lifted the scraggly hair that had grown back in patches around his forehead. A thin, jagged scar marred his hairline.

"I can take care of that."

Eric shrugged. "I'm more interested in repairing this." He lifted his T-shirt and indicated the most severe areas.

Crane studied the scarring. "We can take skin grafts and smooth over the skin. There'll be some residual scarring, but it'll look ten times more normal than now."

He nodded, and glanced at his watch just as the phone rang. Devlin was right on time. He was supposed to create a distraction to lure the doctor out of his office so Eric could search his computer.

"Yes." Crane angled his head to the earpiece. "My car is being towed? Whatever for?" He hesitated. "But I have an assigned spot." Another pause. "I can't believe they're repaving the parking lot during the week." He reached for his keys. "All right, I'll be right there." Crane slammed down the phone and stood. "This is ridiculous. Will you excuse me for a moment? I'll be right back."

Eric nodded. "I'd offer to move it for you, but hey, I brought my wheels with me."

The doctor's eyes narrowed, then an apologetic smile creased his lips. "Right, I shouldn't complain."

He rushed out the door, looking harried. Eric waited until the door closed, then wheeled around the desk and glanced at the computer.

He clicked on the keyboard to access patient files but footsteps quickly returned. Crane hadn't had time to walk downstairs. Damn it. Eric rolled back to the opposite side of the desk, pretending innocence when Crane strode back in.

"That was fast."

"I caught my assistant, had him move the car."

He should have known Crane wouldn't make it easy. He'd have to work on hacking into the system when he returned to his cabin.

AN HOUR AND A HALF LATER, Melissa was about to give up her search. She'd asked about Candace Latone at a local diner, at a craft shop and finally at a real estate agency, but the woman glared at her as if she suspected Melissa might be a stalker. Finally, Melissa drove up and down the island, checking mailboxes, but she didn't locate a single one labeled Latone. Her head was beginning to ache, and her muscles strained from fatigue. The gas gauge on her trusted Camry wobbled to the empty mark and she pulled off at a small gas station. Weary and fearing she'd hit a dead end, she filled the gas tank, then went into the station

to pay. Two old-timers chewing tobacco played check-
ers behind the counter.

She rapped on the counter. "Excuse me, I need to
pay. Fifteen dollars."

A gray-haired man ambled toward her, adjusting his
wiry bifocals. "Thanks, hon."

Melissa nodded. "Listen, I'm looking for someone
and wondered if you could help me."

"Do what I can. I know most people around here."

Early on, Melissa had fabricated a lie, that she was
a long-lost friend of the Latone woman, but that hadn't
worked. Maybe she'd invent another excuse. She introduced herself and learned the man's name was Ho-
mer Wilks. "I'm an insurance agent. I have a check
for a woman named Candace Latone. For some reason,
the printer blurred the address. Could you tell me
where she lives?"

He scratched at the stubble on his chin. "Sure thing.
Twenty-two Cypress Lane. Go past the bluff and turn
left, can't miss it. She lives in a little cottage on the
Wilmington River."

Melissa's heart fluttered. She thanked him, rushed
to her car and drove toward the cottage. The island
was fairly small, the lots filled with trees and well-
tended flower beds, but as she veered onto Cypress,
the beach cottages sprinkled along the streets appeared
to be older and less kept. Palm trees swayed in the
breeze, the telltale signs of age in the vacant weathered
cabins for rent.

Seconds later, she stood at the doorway, inhaling
the scents of the river and flowers on Candace's front
porch, her courage waning as she imagined Candace

Latone's reaction. What if she denied ever giving birth? What if she called the police?

Her pulse racing, she turned to leave, then pivoted around and faced the doorway. A strange thumping sound echoed from inside. Melissa paused and knocked again, waiting with bated breath. Another noise jarred her, like someone scrambling inside, then silence. She knocked again, tapping her foot up and down while she waited, her stomach jitterbugging as she scanned the cottage. Judging from the flower bed in front of the cottage and the row of tulips bordering the front lawn, her mother enjoyed gardening. What else did she like?

She knocked again, but still no answer. Had Candace Latone somehow discovered that she'd come looking for her and decided not to answer the door? Someone was definitely inside.

Melissa hadn't traveled this far to leave without a meeting.

Nerves jangling, she reached for the door and turned the knob. It twisted, and the door swung open, the torn screen slapping in the wind. The hair on the back of her neck prickled. Something didn't feel right. An odd odor permeated the air. A fishy smell—stale air? Blood?

A scent she recognized from old hospital rotations…death.

No, she was letting her imagination go crazy.

The air caught in her lungs. "Miss Latone? Are you here?" Darkness bathed the room, painting it in eerie shadows. The curtains covering the sliding-glass door hung open, the door stood ajar, the night breeze fluttering the sheers. Somewhere in the distance a bird cawed and another screeched in reply. "Is anybody home?"

She tiptoed past the tiny, dark kitchen nook, then around the corner. Her heart constricted. Dear God.

A frail-looking woman lay in a pool of blood on the floor, her eyes gaping open in deathly horror.

Chapter Four

When Eric returned to his cabin, he tried to access the hospital records, but stumbled on a roadblock with security. He'd have to ask Devlin if any of his contacts knew the system. Determined to learn all he could about the research facility, he logged on to the Internet and downloaded all the articles he could find on the companies housed at CIRP. He also earmarked any questionable government hot topics that might correlate between secretive projects on Nighthawk Island to see if he could uncover any possible nets that Hughes might hide beneath.

AIDS research and cloning topped the headlines, with news of successful animal cloning and the controversy over human cloning. Stem cell research was another controversial topic. And of course, chemical and germ warfare experiments.

He'd bet his last dollar the government was conducting biowarfare experiments on Nighthawk Island. Skimming the remainder of the articles, he noted some psychiatric studies under way as well: mind control, projects on treating autism, schizophrenia, bipolar disorder and various psychotic conditions. They had also experimented with a drug to enhance memory loss.

He'd been shocked when Devlin had described Denise Harley's Brainpower research. Of course, he'd read about genetic engineering in the news and shouldn't have been surprised at the scientist's efforts to expand it one step further and create the perfect child. Thankfully, Arnold Hughes would never learn that Simon, the baby Eric's brother and Alanna Hayes were raising as their own, was a product of the experiment *or* that Hughes had actually fathered the baby. If Hughes found out, he'd probably kidnap Simon from Alanna and his brother. Hughes was ruthless. There would be no witnesses left to tell the true story. Or to protect Simon.

He grimaced at the mere idea of using a child in an experiment. Couldn't parents accept their kids and love them for what they were? Did they have to have the perfect child?

Hell, your old man sure didn't think you were perfect.

Apparently, Melissa Fagan's hadn't, either. Had they given her up for adoption because of her seizure disorder, or for other reasons?

MELISSA GASPED, nausea rising to her throat at the sight of the woman's body. Was that Candace Latone? Had she finally located her mother, only to find her dead?

A trembling started deep within her. She had to get help, call someone.

She grabbed her cell phone. Her fingers shook as she dialed 911. "Hello…there's been a shooting."

"Ma'am, what's your name?"

"M-Melissa Fagan, hurry…there's blood, blood everywhere."

"Calm down, take a deep breath, I need an address. Tell me where you are."

Melissa's mind momentarily went blank. She staggered sideways, forcing her gaze away from Candace's bloody body. A sob built in her throat. There was no way the woman could still be alive….

"Ma'am? We need an address."

"Right…uh, Isle of Hope." What street was it? She couldn't think.

Wait. She'd been driving around. Tears dribbled down her cheeks. Her head was spinning. She'd stopped at the gas station…

Spying an envelope on the table, she flipped it over and read, "Candace Latone. Cypress Lane…22 Cypress Lane."

"We'll have an ambulance right there, ma'am. Are you hurt—"

The curtain fluttered. A footstep creaked on the floor behind her. Melissa swung around.

A shadow lunged toward her, then something slammed into her skull, and she fell into darkness.

DARKNESS FELL EARLY on the island, the gray cast covering the sky lowering the spring temperature and adding a chill that Eric found invigorating. Normally he enjoyed being alone, too, had found it peaceful to live in near isolation at the lake. Cain had called him moody.

Now those moods seemed even more acute.

Being alone simply felt lonely.

While he was recovering in the hospital, his brother had insisted the doctors send a counselor to talk to him, some pantywaist shrink who'd encouraged him to express his feelings and deal with residual anger from his youth and his accident. Eric had dismissed the man without even blinking, the black hole of despair dragging him into its clutches.

At the time, his life hadn't meant much to him.

Melissa Fagan's sultry smile floated in his mind, and his gut pinched.

Kissing her—now that would be living.

But he wouldn't be kissing her or doing anything else with her but therapy. Even if his scars didn't repulse her, which they probably would if he made an advance, he couldn't afford to get involved now. If he located Hughes, whoever was near him would be in danger.

He had a new purpose in life—a mission more personal than others, because Hughes had almost killed Eric and his brother.

He grunted and turned on the TV to distract himself. He'd never been much of a couch potato, and had grown even more restless with the mindless crap on the tube while he'd been forced to convalesce. But he kept up with the news.

"Ladies and gentlemen, we bring you this late-breaking story live."

Eric sat up straighter, eyes narrowing at the scene.

"Earlier this evening, a woman identified as Candace Latone was shot to death in her cottage on Isle of Hope." The camera panned the outside of the cottage, showing flowers and a neatly kept yard with an ambulance sitting in the driveway, its lights twirling. Police cars were parked at odd angles in the yard, a half-dozen spectators gathered. "Police are investigating the crime as we speak. A young woman discovered Miss Latone's body, although reports state that she did not see the killer. She was attacked from behind and suffered a mild concussion."

The camera zeroed in on the paramedics hauling a body bag from the scene, then swept to a gurney near the ambulance where paramedics attended the woman who'd found the body. Eric gripped the arms of his wheelchair, his heart pounding.

The woman was Melissa Fagan.

MELISSA'S HEAD ACHED from the questions.

Detective Adam Black knelt beside her. A tough-looking female cop named Bernstein stood beside Black, eyeing Melissa as if she had murdered Candace Latone herself.

"Did you see anything?" Detective Black asked.

"No. The curtain fluttered, then I heard footsteps and someone attacked me from behind." She wrapped the blanket tighter around her shoulders.

"Was Miss Latone still alive when you arrived?" Bernstein asked.

"No... I don't think so." Visions of the splattered blood played before her, and she squeezed her eyes shut to block the images. "There was so much blood, and her eyes…they were wide open."

"Did you touch her?" Detective Black asked.

"No. I was in shock. Then I remember thinking I had to get help, and I reached for my phone."

"Did you touch anything else?" Black asked.

She strained to remember. "Just the door coming in. And…the floor when I fell. I think I hit the end table."

"Yes, with your head," he said gently. "You'll probably have a whopper headache for a while."

Melissa nodded. The police had taken photographs, the M.E. had completed a brief exam, and they'd carried Candace Latone's body to the ambulance. Her mother…or was she? Melissa hadn't even gotten to speak to her, to ask her the truth….

Detective Bernstein's voice turned cold. "What exactly was your relationship to Miss Latone?"

Startled, Melissa glanced away. The lights twirled against the dark sky. Voices hummed in the background. Neighbors had gathered to gawk and speculate. The old man from the gas station who'd given her directions stared at her through squinted eyes.

She cleared her throat, realizing she did look suspicious, and not liking it. "We didn't have one."

"You'd never met?" Bernstein asked.

"No."

Her dark eyebrows rose. "So, what were you doing here?"

Tears welled in Melissa's throat again, but she swallowed them, determined not to cry for a woman who'd abandoned her. But how should she answer the question?

The insurance story trembled on the tip of her tongue, but she couldn't lie to the police. A lie would only incriminate her more.

"Miss Fagan, what were you doing here?" Detective Black asked more gently.

She glanced up, willing them to understand. "I came to meet her. I...had reason to believe she was my m-mother."

Bernstein had been jotting notes in her notepad, but she paused. "Really? How interesting."

Melissa bit her lip, tasting blood and feeling sicker to her stomach by the minute. "I was born here in Savannah, but I was abandoned as a baby. A few months ago, I hired a private investigator to locate my birth parents."

"And he led you here?" Black asked.

"Yes."

Bernstein picked up the questioning. "Had you spoken with Miss Latone on the phone?"

"No."

"She wasn't expecting you?" Bernstein asked, her voice clipped.

"No." Melissa frowned. "At least I don't see how she could. I haven't confided my reasons for coming to Savannah to anyone." Except for Helen.

"How did you find Miss Latone's address?" Bernstein asked.

"A...nurse at the rehab center mentioned that Candace lived on the island. I stopped at the gas station for directions."

Bernstein clicked her pen, in and out, in and out. "Did you tell anyone that you thought Miss Latone was your mother?"

Melissa hesitated, the clicking sound grating on her nerves. "Actually, I did tell the nurse."

The clicking paused. "I thought you said you hadn't confided in anyone."

Melissa shrugged, growing dizzy from the inquisition. "I forgot."

Bernstein's incessant pen clicking began again. "What about the man at the gas station?"

She twisted the edges of the blanket, pulling it tighter as if the fabric could protect her from reality. "I...I said I was an insurance agent, that I came to give Candace a check."

Bernstein smirked. "So, you lied?"

Melissa glanced at the other cop for help, but his expression remained unreadable. "Yes, but..."

"If you lied then, why should we believe you now?"

Her temper flared. "You think I would walk into a woman's house, murder her, then stick around? I'd have to be pretty stupid to do that, wouldn't I, Detective Bernstein?"

"Maybe that was the plan. You thought your story would throw suspicion off of yourself."

They thought she was a cold-blooded killer?

"Young girl, abandoned as a baby, waited all these years to find her mother, then—" Bernstein snapped her fingers for emphasis "—wham, she confronts her, the woman denies she's her mother, and the girl loses her temper."

"That's not true."

Bernstein pushed her face toward Melissa, crowding her. "Maybe she ordered you to get lost, claimed she didn't want you then, and she didn't want you now."

"No, that's not what happened," Melissa cried.

"Why should we believe you?"

"Because I didn't kill her," Melissa said, hysteria rising. "I came here to talk to her, to meet her, that's all. I don't even own a gun."

"That can be checked out." Detective Black held up a warning hand when Bernstein started to pounce on her again. "Miss Fagan, where are you staying?"

"I work at the rehabilitation clinic at CIRP. I live in one of the employee cottages."

The odd look that flashed into Detective Black's eyes surprised her. "You're working at CIRP?"

"Yes. But I've only been there a few weeks." She clutched his arm. "Detective, is there any way you can keep my reasons for being here confidential? I don't want everyone to know that I thought Candace was my mother."

Bernstein resumed the pen clicking. "I doubt that, Miss Fagan. You've just given us a motive for murdering Miss Latone."

ERIC'S NERVES WERE strung tight as he watched the remainder of the news. He recognized two of the cops on the scene, Detective Adam Black and Clayton Fox. Both had been involved with the investigation into CIRP. Black was partly responsible for uncovering the former CEO, Sol Santenelli and Arnold Hughes's original deception.

He had to see if Melissa was okay.

Outside, a spring breeze fluttered the tops of the palm trees and brought the scent of the ocean, along with a fine spray of salty water that brushed his face. He passed three cottages, then approached Melissa's and circled around to the front. He parked beneath the cluster of trees near her entrance and studied the constellations while he waited on her. When he was little, he'd enjoyed watching the stars, but his father had called him a sissy and had broken his telescope in one of his rages. Eric had given up star watching and childish dreams and turned serious.

Now he had to forget dreaming and focus on reality.

Silence hung in the thick, humid air. The ocean tides broke and crashed on the shore. Finally, a car engine cut into the tension, and Melissa's Camry roared up and screeched to a stop. She flicked off the headlights, then opened the car door, her face pale beneath the quarter moon. His gut clenched when he noticed the bruise on her forehead. She seemed unsteady as she walked up the pathway to the door.

"Melissa?"

She startled and jumped back, wide-eyed.

He silently cursed himself for scaring her. "I'm sorry, I didn't mean to frighten you."

She heaved a shaky breath, then fanned her face. "Eric, what are you doing here?"

"I saw the news." He steered the chair toward her. "Are you all right?"

Tears welled in her eyes. He wanted to reach out and touch her. But she stood a foot above him, and he was helpless to do anything but study her. "They said you were assaulted. Are you okay?"

She fumbled in her purse for her keys. "Yes... actually, no, I'm kind of shaken up." The keys rattled in her hands. She dropped them, picked them up and wrestled to insert the key in the door, but her hands were trembling so badly she couldn't manage the task.

He rolled forward and gently took them from her hands. "Here, let me help."

She relented, brushing a strand of hair from her face. He reached for the knob, but the door swung open. "You didn't lock it?"

Panic lit her eyes. "Yes...I did."

Protective instincts surfaced. He motioned for her to wait outside. "I'll check it out."

Melissa grabbed the back of his chair. "No, Eric, you can't go inside."

His jaw snapped tight as he realized her implication. *You're crippled. Helpless. How could you protect me when you can't even walk without assistance?*

Rage exploded inside him. If he couldn't protect a woman, what good was he?

"I said wait here." He hurled the chair forward, pausing to listen for intruders.

"DAMN IT, DID YOU HAVE to kill Candace Latone?" He tugged at his chin in agitation, screwed off the cap to his blood pressure medicine and downed a pill. He'd worked so hard all these years, things couldn't spiral out of control now.

The repercussions from Robert Latone would be harsh.

The other man wheezed over the line. "We can't take any chances. That Fagan woman is here, snooping into things."

"How much does she know?"

"I'm not sure. But she believes Candace was her mother."

"What? This is unreal." He raked a hand across his polished mahogany desk, sending papers scattering. Had Latone lied to him?

"Some Atlanta P.I. gave her Candace's name. He was investigating the research being done back then, too."

"What else does he know?"

"Don't worry about him, he's history."

"Make sure there's no connection." God, what a mess. "And don't get murder happy. The Feds are breathing down our necks already. We can't afford to bring any more suspicion to the center."

"Right. So, you want me to off the Fagan woman?"

"No. Not yet. Just watch her, and find out what she wants."

"And keep her from digging up secrets?"

"Exactly. I don't like her talking to those cops Black and Fox."

"Hey, they suspect she killed Candace. Maybe they'll take care of her for us, lock her up." He chuckled. "If not, maybe Candace's murder will scare her away."

He slammed down the phone. Maybe so.

But if not, well, he'd do whatever he had to do to protect the past.

But he had to wonder—had Latone lied to him?

If so, he'd be sorry....

Chapter Five

Melissa hesitated at the doorway. Even in her disoriented state, she'd insulted Eric Collier's male pride. Yet how could she allow him to enter a potentially threatening situation in his weakened condition, especially to protect her?

Even more unsettling, had someone been inside her cottage? And if so, why?

After the scene at Candace Latone's house, her imagination was running rampant, every horror movie she'd ever seen flitting into her mind. She removed her cell phone from her purse, ready to dial 911, then glanced in the corner, grabbed her umbrella for protection and tiptoed into the cabin. Eric had not bothered to turn on the light. He wheeled into the small den, glancing around the darkened interior, his movements deathly quiet for a man in a wheelchair. Her heartbeat thumped wildly in her chest as she inched up behind him.

He gestured toward the bedroom. His cabin must have been built on a similar plan, because he seemed to know the layout. The kitchen and dining nooks were connected to the small living room, creating an open space, with one bedroom and bath to the side.

She studied the room for anything amiss, and frowned. She hadn't brought very many personal things with her, and hadn't added a single item to make the place homey, choosing to keep the furniture that had come with the cottage. Not that she had any personal family photographs or collectibles to cart around, a sad testament to her lonely existence.

Besides, she'd intended to stay only long enough to get some answers.

Eric pointed to the desk in the corner near the sliding glass doors, and she noticed the drawer ajar. A few of her notes were scattered on the floor, the various files she'd collected from the private investigator tousled through as if someone had searched them.

Her pulse clamored. Someone *had* been here. But why would they be interested in her files?

Because they know why you're in Savannah, and they don't want you to learn the truth....

Dear Jesus. The answer hit her with the force of a fist, nearly robbing her breath. She clutched the wall for support. Eric caught her arm and motioned for her to leave, but she shook her head. He exhaled, then rolled into the bedroom doorway.

She stood behind him, eyeing the room. The navy comforter on the oak bed had been stripped, the closet door open, the meager contents of her wardrobe shuffled as if someone had scavenged through them. But whoever had broken in had already left.

Remembering the tiny handmade bonnet her mother had left her, she raced past Eric to the nightstand where she kept it and threw open the drawer. The lid on the box had shifted. Relief spilled through her at the sight of the small cap. She pressed it to her cheek, the scent of the worn thread and baby softness reminding her of its preciousness.

Eric's hand gently touched hers. "Someone was in here."

She jerked her head up. "I know."

"Do you have any idea why?"

Candace Latone's bloody body flashed into her head. Even if Melissa hadn't shot the gun that had killed Candace, had her quest for the truth about her past caused her mother's death?

What kind of Pandora's box had she opened?

ERIC REALIZED MELISSA saw him as handicapped, but he couldn't tolerate the fear in her pale green eyes or the pain etched on her beautiful face.

He had always been a sucker for a woman in trouble, and although Melissa was tougher than the abused women he'd helped in the past, she was definitely in trouble. At least he could be a friend to her.

She slumped down onto the bed.

He moved the chair closer to her, then tipped her chin up in his palm. "Melissa, talk to me. What's going on?"

She bit down on her lip, then squeezed the crocheted bonnet. "This…it's the only thing I have from my mother."

His gut pinched. Unable to admit he knew she'd been abandoned, he nodded, silently coaching her to continue.

"She dropped me off on the steps of a church when I was only a baby."

"And she left that cap with you?"

A small smile softened the tight lines of her mouth. "Silly for me to keep it, isn't it?"

Eric shook his head and gestured toward his gold cross. "My mother gave me this for my thirteenth birthday. She died not long after."

Melissa smiled, reached out and touched the cross.

He'd also kept the storybook his mother had read to him as a kid, *The Little Engine That Could*. God, how he'd loved that book, how he'd wanted to be that heroic little engine and carry his mother away from her mountain of troubles. But he'd failed and his mother had died.

He couldn't fail Melissa now.

"The woman that was murdered, was she your mother?" he asked quietly.

A small gasp escaped her. "How did you know?"

He shrugged. "Just putting two and two together."

She lowered her head again, a wealth of sadness in the movement. "I didn't even get to talk to her, to ask her." Her lower lip trembled. "She was d-dead when I arrived."

The tears overflowed then, gut-wrenching and honest. Eric had no choice. He pulled her into his arms and held her. Two lost souls clinging together as one for the moment.

"The police think I killed her." The admission gushed out, and Eric rocked her back and forth, soothing her with nonsensical words.

"They'll investigate, find out the truth." He stroked

her hair, inhaling the sweet gardenlike fragrance of her shampoo.

"But what if they don't?" She raised her head, tears streaking her already pale cheeks. "And what if I am responsible?"

His chest ached for her. "You're not responsible."

She shook her head, her eyes wild with panic. "But what if I am? Do you really think it's a coincidence that she's lived here all this time, and the day I show up at her door, she's murdered?" She clutched his hands. "No wonder the police think I killed her."

He cupped her face in his hands, stroking his thumbs along her cheeks. "Shh. Everything's going to be all right."

"But how can it be?" she cried. "I came here looking for her. She died because of me."

"You can't be certain of that, Melissa."

"What other explanation could there be?" Her nails dug into his hands. "Just look around, Eric, someone broke in here and searched through the notes I'd gathered from the private investigator I hired. They wanted to see how much I knew about my mother."

"Maybe," he admitted. "I'm calling Seaside Security, Melissa, to tell them about the break-in. They'll change your locks."

"You think whoever broke in might come back?"

"It's possible, if they didn't find what they wanted tonight." She was shivering when he hung up. Eric pulled her into his arms again, stroking her hair and trying to soothe her.

Her deduction about the Latone woman's murder made sense. If the murderer thought Melissa had uncovered information that might expose him, she was definitely in danger herself.

And why had Candace Latone been murdered? Because of Melissa, or because Candace had been involved in some kind of experiment at the center? What kind of experiment? But why would someone come after her now, years later?

Had she been silenced because she knew something about Melissa's birth that would disrupt the lives of her blood relatives—maybe Melissa's father?

MELISSA SAVORED THE FEEL of Eric's comforting arms, and for a brief few moments leaned into the hard wall of his chest. Closing her eyes, she blocked the images of Candace's eyes bulging in horror and the image of the hole in her chest. Though snatches of the red refused to fade, she inhaled, breathing in the menthol scent of Eric's aftershave and his masculine presence. She had been alone for so very long, had never had a father or any man to shelter her from the horrors of her own nightmarish past.

Unfortunately the nightmare had continued.

Could Eric really understand her feelings? How abandoned and alone she'd been all her life? He carried scars from the accident, but the man still emanated strength.

His arms tightened around her, and she felt a kiss brush her hair. Her stomach fluttered.

Then she angled her head to look up at him and saw a flicker of hunger in his dark brown eyes. Their gazes locked, and an attraction she could no longer deny obliterated the horror of the evening.

As if Eric read her mind, he caressed her cheek with his thumb, then slowly lowered his head a fraction of an inch. She could almost taste his desire, yet he paused as if seeking permission. Swept away by the moment and the feel of his thumb tantalizing her skin, she cupped his jaw in her hand and pulled him toward her. His lips touched hers with such gentle sweetness that she felt something deep inside her tug. Heat radiated through her, unleashing emotions she had never experienced.

The other men in her life had been aggressive. Cold. Had pushed for things she hadn't been ready to give.

Eric, on the other hand, ignited such a yearning in her that she craved more.

He deepened the kiss, and she succumbed, tasting his masculinity as he teased her lips apart and slipped his tongue inside. He threaded his fingers into her hair and she nibbled at his mouth. But the arms of his wheelchair cut into her side, bringing her back to reality.

She had always been alone, had never relied on anyone. She didn't know how to do so now.

Besides, Eric was a patient. Her job mandated she help him, not take advantage of his kindness.

And what about maintaining a professional relationship?

She ended the kiss slowly, the low moan he emitted making it more painful to pull away. She couldn't be his therapist and get involved with him. He was vulnerable, needy right now.

Besides, she had caused one woman's death. What

if the killer came looking for her? She might unwillingly endanger Eric.

Summoning every vestige of restraint she possessed, she released him and stood, then walked to the bedroom doorway. "You'd better go, Eric."

He hesitated. "If that's what you want."

No, it wasn't what she wanted, but it had to be. "Yes, please. I...that shouldn't have happened."

The chair creaked across the floor toward her. Then he was beside her, looking up at her with passion-glazed eyes. And something else—a shadow of vulnerability.

"Because I'm like this?" Anger hardened his voice as he gestured down at his battered legs.

"Partly."

Hurt shadowed his face, a self-deprecating laugh following. "At least you're honest."

"Don't take it the wrong way, Eric." For goodness' sake, would she have allowed him to kiss her like that if she wasn't attracted to him? She hated to cause him further pain, but he had to understand they couldn't indulge in a relationship that had no future. She might be leaving soon, and when he learned to walk again, he would return to his life. "I'm supposed to be a professional, Eric." She inhaled sharply. "But if you want, I can get another therapist assigned to you."

"I don't want another therapist, Melissa. I want you."

A tingle traveled up her spine at his husky voice. But the security agency arrived, preventing any further discussion. Eric explained what had happened, then he took one last look at her and wheeled across the room.

"Lock the doors. And call me if you need anything."
Then he disappeared into the night, the sound of his
wheelchair creaking across the pavement.

She pressed her fingers to her mouth, trying to get
a grip so she could talk to the police. His parting
words were imprinted in her brain just as his kiss had
been imprinted on her lips.

Why had she met him now when they couldn't possibly have a relationship…?

ERIC CURSED HIMSELF the entire way back to his cottage. He shouldn't have kissed Melissa, shouldn't have
taken advantage of the situation. Just because he was
needy, and it had been forever since he'd touched a
woman, and he had irrational, lustful thoughts of his
therapist, didn't mean she viewed him in a sexual way.

He glared at his battered legs, a visible reminder of
how little he had to offer.

Melissa Fagan was a beautiful woman. A whole
woman who needed a whole man.

And even when he could walk, he hadn't been
whole.

She'd been alone all her life. She certainly deserved
to have a man who could give her everything, his
body, his soul and a bright future.

Eric had lost all three.

Wheeling into his room, he still couldn't shake the
worry. She had found a dead woman tonight, a woman
she believed was her mother. Then someone had broken into her place.

Someone who knew she'd been searching for her
parents.

But why kill Candace Latone?

He watched the evening news, but the police offered no more details on the Latone murder than they had earlier, although the camera panned to a live interview. Thankfully, they didn't mention the break-in at Melissa's.

"Mr. Latone," the reporter said. "I know you must be shocked to hear of your daughter's death."

"I'm devastated. She was my only child." Latone raised his chin, anger gleaming in the depths of his pain-filled eyes. "And I will make sure that whoever killed my daughter pays. Now—" his voice broke "—I'd like to be alone."

He hurried toward his limousine, and the camera zoomed back to the reporter. "That was Robert Latone, a foreign diplomat for the U.S. government, whose daughter was murdered tonight. If you have any information that might lead to the killer, phone your local police."

Eric frowned as he watched the limousine drive away. If Candace Latone was Melissa's mother, then Robert Latone was her grandfather. Had he known about Melissa?

He phoned Luke Devlin. "It's Eric. What do you know about the Latone woman's murder?"

"Why are you interested?"

"Melissa Fagan, the woman who found the body, thinks Candace Latone was her birth mother."

A heartbeat of silence passed. "I see."

"Someone also broke into Melissa Fagan's cottage and searched through the files from the P.I."

"Interesting. Did she mention anything about her birth father?"

"No. But she blames herself for the Latone woman's death. And apparently, at least one of the cops who questioned her suspects she killed Candace."

"She does have motive."

"She's not a killer."

Devlin hissed into the silence. "Don't get involved with her, Eric. She might be a bigger part of this whole case than we thought."

"What do you mean? Is there something you're not telling me?"

Another hesitation. "No, but the coincidences are too strong. Anyone who knew Hughes or was at the center when he was employed has to be treated with suspicion. And Candace Latone's father, Jack Latone, has donated money to CIRP."

"Melissa didn't kill Candace Latone," Eric said again. "But she might be in danger."

"Right. Or she might be lying. Don't let a pretty face sucker punch you." Devlin whistled. "Use her, warm up to her, maybe she can help you gain access to the computer security system so we can hack into restricted files."

The idea of using Melissa sent a sour taste to Eric's mouth.

Devlin continued, oblivious, "I'll apprise the locals, Detectives Black and Fox, of the situation, and fill them in on your undercover role at CIRP. They both have vested interests in locating Hughes. Perhaps they'll know if there's a connection between Hughes and Candace Latone or her father.''

''Right. And maybe Black and Fox will find evidence of the real killer,'' Eric added.

And something to exonerate Melissa.

MELISSA CHECKED the locks on the small cottage a half-dozen times. The headache that had been threatening all night had grown in intensity since Eric had left. She felt at least marginally safe while he'd been with her, but alone, the shadows screamed at her with self-incriminations, and flashes of blood red appeared before her eyes.

She needed sleep or she might have a seizure.

Restless, she swallowed one of the prescription pills the doctor had given her to help her relax at the onslaught of an episode, praying it would knock her out. Adding a cup of hot tea to the routine, she settled down in bed with a copy of a medical journal, hoping the newest techniques in rehabilitation for shoulder injuries might calm her.

But the words blurred on the page, and Eric's last comment reverberated in her mind.

When he had said he wanted her, had he meant as his therapist or did he mean he wanted *her*?

It doesn't matter. He's a patient. You cannot get involved with him. And if you did, and he was hurt, you'd never forgive yourself.

It's bad enough your search caused your mother's death….

The phone trilled, jarring her from the suffocating guilt. Half hoping it was Eric, but worried it might be that burly cop who'd all but accused her of killing Candace, she hesitated before answering. "Hello."

"Miss Fagan?"

The voice sounded muffled, distant. Not Eric. Maybe the cop?

"Yes? Who is this?"

"If you don't want to end up like Candace Latone, you'd better stop snooping around and leave town."

Melissa gasped. "Who is this?"

The phone clicked in response, then the line went dead, the beep of the dial tone blaring into the night.

Chapter Six

Eric woke feeling agitated, but eager for therapy.

Or maybe he was eager to see his therapist.

He dismissed the thought, reminding himself he had taken a step the day before. Today he would take another and another until he was free of that damn chair, and he could walk on his own two feet. His mobility meant he was closer to independence. To claiming back his life. To answers. To Hughes.

And to being able to protect Melissa.

After breakfast, he called Cain, as promised, to relay his progress. Cain was ecstatic.

"I never doubted you'd recover," Cain said. "But I hate that you've had to go through all this."

"How's Alanna and the baby?"

"Great. You should hear Simon, he's only a few months old and babbling like a toddler."

Eric laughed, his first true one in weeks. They had suspected Simon had superior intelligence due to the experiment. It must be true.

"How about you, man? I know the therapy's tough."

Eric shrugged it off, and relayed the events about the Latone murder and Melissa.

"Keep your eyes and ears peeled," Cain said. "Devlin could be right. Melissa Fagan might be a trap."

"She's not," Eric said emphatically. "But I'll stay on my toes."

A tense silence stretched between them, but Eric chuckled. "It was a joke, bro. I'm really all right."

Cain sighed, still sounding worried, but Eric told him to kiss his new wife and baby for him, then hung up and headed to the rehab center. As soon as he spotted Melissa inside, his adrenaline kicked in, along with worry and a tingly sensation that he recognized as arousal. He hadn't experienced the feeling in such a long time, he'd almost forgotten how all-powerful sexual attraction could be.

He not only found Melissa physically desirable, but he admired her strength and tenacity in overcoming her own disability, and her pursuit of the truth about her ugly past.

There was no way she could have murdered Candace Latone.

A young woman who'd been alone all her life, who'd come seeking the truth about her mother, wouldn't have killed her only known parent without giving her the opportunity to forge a relationship.

But what if the Latone woman had flatly denied she was Melissa's mother? What if she'd denied wanting any part of her? Could she have driven Melissa to desperation?

Had he been snowed by the shadows of old hurts in her eyes?

No...

The cops had obviously jumped on that train of thought, looking for the easiest person to collar for the crime instead of delving deeper for a killer in disguise. He understood the art of deception.

He was a fake himself.

He couldn't even reveal his real name, or offer to help Melissa with the police. And he couldn't jeopardize the case by getting so sidetracked with her problems or his lust for her that he forgot the mission.

Could the two be connected in any way?

He had tossed the idea back and forth all night. As he approached Melissa, he channeled his energy into his physical regimen.

His job, his life, Melissa's life, might depend on his recovery.

MELISSA HADN'T SLEPT at all the night before. The threatening phone call had played over and over in her mind, as had the images of Candace's dead body and the guilt that she had caused her own mother's death. And even when she'd reported the call, she'd sensed the police hadn't believed her.

If you don't want to end up like Candace Latone, you'd better stop snooping around and leave town.

She wasn't leaving. But what would she do if the killer attacked her? What didn't he want her to find? Her father?

Helen practically accosted her when she arrived. The nurse had watched the news and felt horrible, as if she thought she might be responsible for leading Melissa to Candace's house to kill her. Melissa had assured Helen that she wasn't a murderer, that she had desperately wanted to meet the woman who'd given her life and was crushed over being deprived of the opportunity.

"Good morning, Melissa."

She said goodbye to her other patient and turned toward Eric, bracing herself against a reaction. Memories of the kiss they'd shared the night before lingered in her mind.

From the way his dark eyes raked over her, he hadn't forgotten, either.

"Are you ready to get started?"

"Yes."

She nodded and they fell into their warm-up routine. More patients came in, working with Helen and two other therapists, while Nancy assisted. Melissa let the sight and sounds of the others distract her from indulging her fantasies of Eric, at the same time warning Eric not to overdo the workout. The small step the day before had fueled his determination and physical strength.

He was far more resilient and tougher than any of her former patients. Or any of the previous men in her life.

The night before, he'd been tender. Gentle. Understanding. He even knew about her condition and hadn't gone running....

He's not in your life, he's your patient.

Besides, what did she really know about the man and his former life? His chart stated that he owned a ranch in the North Georgia mountains, but he never spoke about it. And he didn't look like a rancher....

Questions and doubts assailed her as she coaxed him through the warm-up routine, punishing stretches and pressure exercises. When he gripped the bars, the veins in his arms bulged as they shook with the effort to stand and move his feet forward, and she had to tear her eyes from his sexy physique.

Finally, after taking several steps on his own, Melissa insisted he rest. "You can try again later if you want, but you don't want to have a setback, do you?"

His mouth tightened. "No."

She patted his arm, aware the muscle flexed beneath her touch. "You worked hard today, you're making progress. You'll be walking with a cane in no time."

A long sigh escaped him, pent with frustration and acceptance. "You look tired. You didn't sleep?"

Odd, how she'd commented the same thing to him on several occasions. "I couldn't stop thinking about Candace."

Eric settled into his wheelchair and swiped at perspiration on his forehead. "And the intruder?"

She nodded, avoiding his eyes. "Are you ready for the whirlpool?"

Hoping to avoid any more questions, she stepped aside so he could wheel his way over, but he caught her hand. "Did something else happen last night, Melissa?"

Her fingers curled into a fist. "I...no."

"You're a terrible liar," he said in a low, almost intimate voice. "What is it?"

She bit down on her lip, remembering the sweet

serenity of Eric's mouth upon hers. Heaven help her, but she craved that comfort again, that closeness.

"Tell me, Melissa."

"I...received a phone call."

"From whom?"

She shrugged, the fine hairs on the back of her neck prickling. "I don't know."

"What did the caller say, Melissa?"

She swallowed bile at the thought of the man's husky threat. "He warned me to stop snooping around and leave town or else."

His dark eyes bored into hers. "Or else what?"

"Or else I'd end up like Candace."

A STEELY RAGE HARDENED Eric's mouth. Melissa had masked her fear with a brave face, but terror haunted her eyes. "Did you call the police?"

"Yes, but I'm not sure they believed me."

"What are you going to do?"

She tucked a strand of hair back into her ponytail. "I'm not running."

"Maybe you should."

She gestured toward the whirlpool. "I can't leave now, not without knowing who killed my mother and why."

"Let the police handle it, Melissa. You don't understand what you're up against." Or maybe she didn't care. He saw the desolation in her eyes and realized it was going to cause her to act recklessly.

"It's not your problem, Eric." She gripped his arm to help him stand, but he shook her hand away. "You need to focus on getting better. I can take care of my own problems.''

He grabbed her hand. "What are you planning to do?"

She shrugged. "I told you it's not your problem."

"I'm making it my problem," he said in a deep voice. "Now, tell me your plans."

"I thought about going to Candace's father, but then he might not know Candace had a baby."

"True."

A moment's hesitation lapsed between them, then she finally replied, "I'd like to look inside Candace's house. Maybe there's something there that will give me insight into her life."

"And your own?"

"Yes…" She looked away. "I have to know about her family, the reason she gave me away. About my father."

The real reason she couldn't leave. Her need to investigate her parentage had driven her this far. It was an obsession that would keep driving her.

But would it drive her straight into her own grave?

Melissa checked her watch. "Now, Eric, relax in the whirlpool. I have another patient to see."

He glanced at the door and noticed a man in his mid-fifties wheeling toward her. The young candy striper had commented that the patient was a war vet who'd lost his leg to diabetes. Melissa was helping him learn to adjust to the prosthetic leg.

But Eric couldn't let her leave yet. "Promise me one thing."

"What?" She folded her arms across her chest, and

he remembered the feel of her against his body. His sex hardened, began to ache. The sensations spurred his determination to walk even more. Her gaze caught his sudden arousal, and she shifted, ignoring his reaction, while he lowered himself into the water.

"Promise me that you won't go to the Latone woman's house by yourself."

"Eric—"

"Promise me," he insisted. "It's too dangerous, Melissa." He trapped her with his eyes. "Besides, if the police find you snooping alone, they might think you've returned to the scene of the crime to hide something from them."

He saw her waver, realize he was right. She finally nodded, although her frown spoke volumes. "I'll see if Helen will ride out there with me."

"No. I'll go."

"Eric—"

"Don't insult me again by suggesting that I might not be able to help because I'm in this chair."

She opened her mouth to argue, but her next patient rolled toward her and prevented her reply.

GUILT NIGGLED AT ERIC for misleading Melissa. He wanted to accompany her to protect her, but he also needed to wheedle any information out of her he could. If Candace Latone had been connected to CIRP or Hughes in any way, the connection might be hidden somewhere in the past she'd so obviously tried to bury.

How Melissa played into that was anybody's guess, but a few possibilities raced through his mind, none of which he hoped were true. All of which might prove dangerous to her.

By tagging along with her, he could ensure her safety and explore those possibilities.

His chat with Fox had proved enlightening, as well. Fox relayed the details of the memory transplant experiment the doctors had performed on him, and suggested that the center was working on other experimental brainwashing techniques, possibly in conjunction with the government. He suspected a contact in the FBI was overseeing the project with the intentions of using the techniques in warfare.

A very likely probability, Eric thought. But what exactly did the experiments entail?

He ate an early dinner at the cafeteria where he noticed Ian Hall, the new CEO, eating with Wallace Thacker, the chemist who'd recently come on board at CIRP. One of the men might be Hughes. But which one?

So far Ian Hall had remained low-key, avoiding the press and extra media attention. He'd held one press conference that stated his mission for CIRP was to expunge the negative publicity surrounding the center and build it into the greatest research facility in the world. The reason he'd brought in Thacker. More renowned scientists from around the world would follow. A bone specialist named Steve Crayton had also been hired, but his age and body build didn't fit Hughes's profile.

Melissa met him just as he finished his coffee. "I'm going now."

"Don't you want to eat first?"

She flattened a hand over her stomach. "I'm not hungry. I'll grab something later."

He trailed her to the door.

"Eric, are you sure about this?"

He nodded. Hall was watching them, so Eric made a mental note to talk to the man the next day.

Melissa walked to the passenger side of her Camry and started to open the door, but he shook her hand off. "I can do it myself."

A small smile played on her mouth. "All right."

Using his upper-body strength, he hauled himself over to the seat, reached out and began to fold the chair. Melissa stood watching patiently, then stored it in the trunk of the car.

Leaving the confines of the center and the chair invigorated him. He almost felt normal. As if he was a man on a date with a beautiful woman for the night.

Until they turned onto the street leading to Candace Latone's house, and he saw the yellow crime-scene tape enveloping the house. Melissa's harsh intake of breath cemented reality.

This was not a date for either of them. He was on a mission, and she had come to learn about the woman who'd abandoned her shortly after her birth.

He couldn't forget it, either.

NERVES FLUTTERED in Melissa's stomach as she parked the car and handed Eric the wheelchair. Thankfully, Candace's small cottage had been built on flat ground, eliminating the need for steps. Even though Eric was in a wheelchair, she felt safer simply having him along.

The man's voice from the phone call the night before echoed in her mind.

She would not allow him to scare her. And if her mother had been killed because of Melissa's search, she wanted the killer caught.

The sound of the ocean breaking on the shore filled the night, along with the scent of the marsh and Candace's flowers. Eric followed her to the door, waiting behind her.

"It's locked?" Eric asked.

Melissa jiggled the door and nodded. "I'll go around and check the back and windows."

"There's no need," Eric said. "I'm sure the police secured the premises when they left. Do you have a credit card?"

She nodded and removed a Visa card from her purse. Within seconds, he unlocked the door.

"We could get arrested for breaking and entering, Eric. And I am a suspect."

"That's true." He paused. "We don't have to go in."

"I know." She hesitated. "But I have to learn more about Candace." He offered no explanation about his breaking-in skills, either, and she quickly forgot the question when the scent of death assaulted her.

Melissa reached for the overhead light, but Eric shook his head. "It might arouse suspicion to the neighbors."

She nodded, and dropped her hand, scanning the small living area. Through the haze of filtered moonlight from the sliding-glass doors, she noticed fingerprint dust on the pine end table, saw the chalky line and tape marking the floor where Candace's body had been found. The furniture was sparse and simple. A dark green leather sofa, white-pine coffee table and end tables, fresh flowers in a crystal vase on the glass-top kitchen table in the corner eating nook. Flowers from Candace's own yard. They were already wilting.

She would take fresh flowers to her grave.

A small desk occupied the corner near the sliding-glass doors. On the opposite side, a narrow hall led to what she assumed was the bedroom and bath. Eric parked himself by the sofa and remained silent while she walked into the kitchen.

"I know it's silly," she said quietly as she rummaged through the cabinets, "but I want to see her dishes, her clothes, anything that might tell me something about her."

"It's not silly," Eric said, his voice slightly throaty. "Details reveal a lot about a person."

She removed a handcrafted colorful mug, then turned it over to study the bottom. "It has her initials carved on the bottom. I wonder if she made this herself."

"It's a possibility." Eric gestured toward a whimsical painting on the wall, a watercolor of the ocean and colorful sea creatures in a world of muted blues. "Her signature's on this painting, too."

"She was an artist." Melissa studied the painting. "She was actually pretty good. I wonder if she ever sold any of her work."

"You could check local galleries."

"Maybe I will." She glanced at the bedroom. "I'm going to look around in there."

He nodded. "I'll wait here."

She offered him a watery smile, grateful he understood that she needed some privacy, and walked into the bedroom. More paintings adorned the walls, some swatches of bright colors, full of animation and light. Others were dark, gray, moody shadows of another side of Candace that must have reflected her mental instability.

So far she'd seen no sign of her mother's needlework, that she might have crocheted the tiny cap that belonged to Melissa.

She opened the wooden chest at the foot of the bed and looked inside, hoping it held knitting yarn or crochet hooks and patterns, but linens filled the chest instead. Disappointed, she pivoted to the closet, opened the door and studied Candace's clothes. Like the paintings, her closet held a hodgepodge of bright colors and casual sundresses, capri pants and blouses, then a contrasting selection of dark, drab shirts and black slacks. A hatbox that had been pushed way back on the top shelf drew her eye, and she removed it, then sat on the edge of the corner rocker to survey the contents.

A handful of old letters, scribbled in near-illegible handwriting lay inside. Melissa felt as if she was violating Candace's privacy by touching them, but she couldn't stop herself.

Had the police searched these things? Read her letters?

She skimmed the first one.

Dear Baby,

I miss you so much. Today would have been your first birthday. I wonder if you're walking

now, and talking, if you're calling another
woman Mama. You're probably in a better place,
but I miss you so. I had the nurse bring me a
cupcake today with a candle in it, and I lit the
candle and sang "Happy Birthday" to you, my
angel. Then I closed my eyes and wished that I
would see you again. Maybe one day soon, if I
ever leave this place…

Love,
Your mama

Melissa swiped at the tears running down her
cheeks. Had Candace written the letter to her?

And if she'd intended to find her baby when she
was released from the hospital, why had she never
followed through?

WHILE MELISSA LOOKED around in the bedroom, Eric
rolled over to the desk. Black and Fox had no doubt
searched the contents, but he'd check it out himself in
case they missed something.

The top drawer contained insurance papers, bills, all
the mundane pieces of a person's life. The second
drawer held colorful pens and stationery, along with a
book on calligraphy. He shuffled through the third
drawer, discovering several sketches of the ocean and
sea creatures, then a box of old photos. A quick glance
revealed pictures of seashells, birds, another slice of
her artistic personality come alive.

No family or photos of a loving dad, a boyfriend or
a baby.

He stuffed the box back into the drawer; then noticed a lone picture wedged between the back of the drawer and the edge of the desk.

Curious, he yanked the photo free and held it up to the light. The picture captured the image of five men standing side by side, all in front of the original Savannah Hospital twenty-plus years ago. Eric recognized Sol Santenelli and Arnold Hughes from the photos the Feds had shown him. The third man wore an army uniform. The fourth man resembled the current CEO of CIRP, although Hall supposedly had no former ties to Hughes.

Hall was definitely not Hughes resurfaced. But he had obviously known him.

The fifth man was Robert Latone, meaning Latone also had ties with Hughes early on.

He searched the desk again, and discovered a second photo trapped between the wooden edges. He released it, swallowing hard at the sight of Hughes and Candace Latone together, Hughes's arm draped affectionately around Candace's shoulders.

Candace had supposedly been involved in a research experiment at the center when she'd become pregnant. And she'd known Hughes. Had they been involved?

Could Hughes possibly be Melissa's father?

Chapter Seven

Eric's imagination had run away with him. Melissa's father could have been any one of a hundred men. In order to pinpoint his identity, he'd have to investigate all the men Candace might have been involved with. And if she'd gotten pregnant through a sperm donor, as had Simon's surrogate mother, the possibilities were endless and would require DNA checking as well as an investigation into the experimental project at the time.

Which was an entirely different case.

Yet, if Melissa was Hughes's daughter, he could use her to get to Hughes....

No, he couldn't even contemplate such a possibility.

Melissa entered the room, the misery in her eyes wrenching his gut. She was an innocent in this situation, had searched for her mother only to find her dead. How would she feel about a cold-blooded murderer like Hughes fathering her?

Deciding to explore the possibility before turning her already fragile world upside down with his suspicions, he slid the picture he'd found in Candace's desk into his pocket.

Melissa cleared her throat. "You were looking through the desk?"

"Just trying to help."

She fidgeted with her fingers. "Did you find anything?"

He shook his head. "More art supplies. What about you?"

She nodded. "Some old letters."

"Did they confirm that Candace was your mother?"

Her lip trembled as she nodded. "Candace wrote them to her baby. She…missed me and wanted me back."

Eric's heart squeezed with compassion—and guilt over lying to her. He held out his hand to comfort her, but she shrugged it away. "Come on, let's get out of here."

He nodded and followed her to the car. If Candace was Melissa's mother, had she given her away out of choice or had someone forced her to?

MELISSA'S HEART THROBBED as she drove back to Skidaway Island. All her life she'd ached for her mother, wondered where she was and why she hadn't wanted her. Now, to realize her mother *had* wanted Melissa, had celebrated her birthdays, was a blessing. Yet it intensified the sadness.

She had been so close to meeting Candace, to being reunited. If she'd only arrived at the house a few minutes earlier, she might have been able to save Candace.

Eric laid a hand over hers. "Are you all right?"

No, she wasn't all right. "I…just need some time alone."

"I can understand that." Hadn't he wanted to shut himself away from everything and everyone after the explosion?

She parked in front of his cabin, then hopped out to retrieve his chair. He unfolded it, slid onto the seat, then looked up at her. "Are you sure you want to be alone? We could talk."

Determined not to break down and cry in front of him, she shook her head. "Thanks, but I'm pretty tired. And you need some rest, too."

His mouth tightened.

"Thanks for going with me, Eric. I appreciate it."

He nodded, but hesitated as if he wanted to say more. As if he wanted more.

She remembered the fiery kiss they'd shared the night before and craved another. But she felt so fragile and in need of comfort. If she relented to one kiss, she might lose control and succumb to more. Starting a relationship, even a short-lived one, definitely wouldn't be fair to Eric.

Besides, she couldn't allow herself to rely on anyone, especially a man with problems of his own. So, she said good-night, then climbed into her car alone.

When she pulled up to her cottage, a black limousine was parked in the driveway. For a moment, she remembered the threatening caller the night before. But if her visitor meant her harm, why arrive in something as conspicuous as a limousine?

Still, she removed her cell phone from her purse and held on to it as a safety net. The limo's door opened, a driver exited and opened the back door. An austere, tall, gray-haired man in a dark pin-striped suit emerged. He had a broad angular face with wide cheekbones and a neatly trimmed beard. His demeanor immediately suggested wealth and power. "Miss Fagan?"

She climbed out of the car, but remained in close proximity to the door. How had he known her name? "Yes."

"My name is Robert Latone. Are you the woman who discovered my daughter's body?"

Melissa swallowed. This man was Candace's father?

That would make him her grandfather.

"Yes."

"May I come in and talk to you for a moment?"

Melissa's breath caught, but she nodded, then walked up the driveway and opened the door. The driver slid back into the car to wait, and Robert Latone followed her, his clipped steps on the sidewalk echoing like a soldier's measured pace.

When they entered, she gestured toward the sofa. He declined and shoved his hands into his trouser pockets. A play on power she assumed. She'd dealt with men and power issues in her foster-care homes before. She hadn't caved then, and she wouldn't now. Even if this man was her grandfather.

"Would you like some coffee? Tea?"

"No, thank you. This isn't exactly a social visit."

"I see." Animosity radiated from him in waves. She claimed a wing chair, forcing herself to make eye contact. Did he know she thought Candace was her mother?

"Tell me what you saw at my daughter's cottage."

"I already gave a full report to the police, Mr. Latone."

"You didn't see her killer?"

"No."

"What exactly did you see?"

"The door was open, so I went in. It was getting dark. I noticed the curtains fluttering in the breeze, the sliding-glass door was ajar. Then I saw m...her body." She paused, the images darting back in horrid snippets. "She was already dead."

"What did you do then?"

"I called 911, but someone attacked me from behind." She pressed a hand to her chest, the horror returning. "When I regained consciousness, the paramedics and police were there."

His thin lips creased downward. "My daughter didn't have many friends, Miss Fagan. How did you know her?"

Melissa twisted her hands in her lap, then realized he'd noticed and would read the movement as a sign of weakness, so she fisted them instead. "I didn't, we never met."

Surprise registered on his face a second before suspicion. "Then what were you doing at her house?"

She debated whether to tell him. But if she was his granddaughter, he might already know. And even if he did, he might not acknowledge her....

"I was abandoned when I was a baby, Mr. Latone. I came to Savannah in search of my mother."

Gray eyes bored into hers. "What does that have to do with my daughter?"

Melissa cleared her throat. "I hired a private investigator to find my birth parents. He told me that Candace was my mother."

Shock flared in his tightly reined jaw, then anger. "He was mistaken. My daughter never had a baby. I can have her medical records pulled to prove it." His voice turned hard, brittle. "And if you spread such ill rumors, I'll sue you for slander."

With one last warning look, he strode out the door, slamming it behind him. Melissa heard the soft purr of the limousine's engine, then shells spraying from the wheels as it disappeared into the night.

Had Candace not told her father about the baby, or was it possible that Candace hadn't delivered a child? Melissa had read the letters Candace had written. Unless, in her illness, Candace had invented the baby....

Had Robert Latone been telling the truth?

A SOON AS ERIC returned to the cabin, he called Devlin and filled him in on the photograph.

"I'm sending our local contacts over to look at it," Devlin said. "Good work."

Eric hung up, a sour taste in his mouth. Good work—only he was keeping secrets from Melissa, secrets that involved her, secrets that might lead her to the answers she'd been seeking for years.

Unfortunately she might not like the answers.

Within the hour, Detectives Black and Fox arrived at his door.

"Agent Devlin said you found a photograph?" Black said without preamble.

"Yeah." Eric gestured for them to follow him to the living area. The layout mirrored Melissa's, the furniture utilitarian and sturdy, although his had been built with added handicapped accommodations.

He removed the photograph from the desk and handed it to Black. Fox sidled up to him so they could both study it.

"It's Hughes, Santenelli, Robert Latone, Candace Latone's father and the new CEO, Ian Hall. I'm not sure who the other man is," Eric said.

"Which means the new CEO is not Hughes," Fox said.

"It seems that way," Eric said.

"We'll see what we can find out on the other man," Black added.

"What do you know about Robert Latone?" Eric asked.

"He's a foreign diplomat," Black said. "So far, he's donated several million dollars to CIRP since its conception years ago."

"There's been speculation that he might be involved in espionage," Fox added.

Eric whistled through his teeth. "Do you have any idea what type of research experiment Candace Latone was involved in?"

"We're not sure, but there was some kind of scandal involving a fertility specialist," Black said. "He left the country before things were cleared up." Two fertility specialists had been involved in creating Simon.

''The psychological problems the Latone woman experienced might have been related to the experimental research,'' Fox added. ''But details have been kept hush-hush.''

Black narrowed his eyes, studying the photograph. ''Wait a minute, are you thinking what I am?'' He cut his gaze toward Eric. ''You think there's a tie to the recent experiments with Project Simon?''

''How did you know about Simon?'' Eric asked.

''Devlin filled us in,'' Fox said.

''Hughes can't find out about Simon,'' Eric said. ''He'd ruin my brother's life as well as the baby's.''

''You don't have to worry,'' Fox said. ''The information goes no further than the three of us.''

Eric nodded, still anxious.

''Do you think this all ties back to Melissa Fagan?'' Black asked.

''I don't know.'' Eric scrubbed a hand over his face. ''She was born at the center. And Candace and Hughes seem chummy in the photo.''

Fox cleared his throat. ''You think Hughes might be Melissa Fagan's father?''

MELISSA WAS SO SHAKEN by Robert Latone's visit that she'd barely slept the night before. Candace would be buried today. Melissa had planned to attend. Now she didn't know what to do.

She grabbed a bagel and hurried to the rehab center, anxious to see Eric. Her therapy sessions would distract her from her problems, and she was excited by Eric's quick progress. Before the week ended, he'd be using a walker, maybe even a cane.

The sight of Eric's masculine body wheeling toward her sent heat exploding within her. Heat that had nothing to do with therapy sessions and work, but with the sexual chemistry brewing between them.

Even more unsettling, she felt safe with him. A feeling she had never experienced in her life, especially with a man.

"Good morning." She automatically assumed the pattern they'd established in the beginning for the warm-up stretching exercises. Eric was one step ahead of her, already propping his foot on the apparatus and flexing his calf. He seemed tense this morning.

"Did you have nightmares about the accident again last night?"

Eric shrugged. "I'm not sure if they'll ever go away."

She massaged his calf, then knelt and braced herself to help through the routine. "You want to talk about it?"

"Another man died in the accident," he said, his voice strained.

She hesitated. "A friend of yours?"

"Sort of. He was in trouble, I was trying to help him out."

"I'm sorry."

"It's not your fault."

But he blamed himself. She offered a feeble smile. "I know, but I'm still sorry. His death must haunt you." She coached him to the next level of the set. "You want to tell me how the accident happened?"

A mask slipped over his face, guarded, void of emotions. Or at least he wanted to hide them. But a deep pain settled in his eyes. "Maybe another time."

"All right."

"How about you?" he asked as she helped him stand and move to the bars. "Did you dream about your mother's murder?"

"No, but I didn't sleep, either." Melissa glanced down at his feet, urging him to take a step forward. "I had a visitor last night."

Eric gripped the bars and paused, searching her face. "The person who threatened you?"

She shook her head. "No, Robert Latone, Candace's father."

Eric remained still, waiting. "What did he want?"

"To find out if I'd seen anything that might help identify Candace's killer."

"Did he mention your relationship to Candace?"

She urged him to continue the drill, and he stepped forward. One step. Two steps. Three. Four. They were coming easier now, his brain and body beginning to heal and work together. "He denied that Candace had a child and threatened to sue me if I spread rumors."

Compassion softened Eric's expression, tightening the knot of unshed tears in Melissa's throat.

"Melissa, I'm sorry. But there are tests that can be run."

"Right." Melissa patted his hand, silently urging him through the workout. "I'll think about it. Although I doubt Robert Latone will cooperate. And if Candace's DNA has to be provided, he'll probably protest."

Eric nodded and they completed the session.

The young candy striper suddenly appeared. "Melissa, two police officers are in the office requesting to talk to you."

Melissa's breath caught. "All right, can you help Mr. Collier over to the whirlpool?"

"I can manage," Eric said in a gruff voice. He pushed Nancy's hands away when she reached out to offer assistance. Melissa smiled at his stubborn independence.

But nerves bunched in her stomach as she headed to the office. Had the police found her mother's murderer?

Or had they come to arrest her?

ERIC HAD NO IDEA WHY he'd confided in Melissa about the accident. He couldn't confess the truth, though, without revealing more about his identity and the reasons for being at CIRP.

He hated lying to her.

Ironic that after a lifetime of helping and protecting women, he now had to hide from the first woman he was interested in.

She couldn't be Hughes's daughter.

Maybe Latone was right. Maybe she wasn't Candace Latone's daughter, either.

And maybe you'll get married and ride away into the sunset on your ranch like they do in the movies.

He wiped his forehead with the gym towel, ignoring the candy striper who still couldn't bring herself to look at his ugly scars. Not that he blamed her. A pretty young girl like her should be protected from the grotesque violence of the world.

But no one had been there to protect Melissa.

Sliding himself from the chair, he braced his body using the rails and slowly lowered himself to the first step of the whirlpool. He eased into the water from there with no problem. He was getting stronger every day.

But would he be strong enough to protect Melissa if she needed him? What if the person who'd threatened her decided to carry out those threats?

Maybe he should try to convince her to drop the search for her parents, at least until he could finish the investigation, locate Hughes and lock him away. Then he'd help her.

He glanced toward the glass doors leading to the inner offices of the rehab center. Had the police caught her mother's killer?

FIVE MINUTES LATER, Melissa sat in the office, squeezing a tepid cup of hospital coffee between her hands, facing Detectives Black and Fox. Thankfully the gestapo-like Bernstein had not accompanied them.

"Miss Fagan, we need to ask you a few more questions." Black occupied the vinyl chair across from her, while Detective Fox stood, sipping a cup of coffee.

Something about Detective Black's tone triggered alarm in her belly. "Do I need a lawyer?"

He arched an eyebrow. "Not unless you have something to hide."

Her jaw tightened. "I told you I didn't kill Candace Latone. I'll do whatever I can to assist with the investigation."

"Good, we appreciate your cooperation," Black said.

Fox cleared his throat. "Miss Fagan, do you know Robert Latone?"

Melissa's head jerked up. "No. Well, not exactly."

The officers waited, and she clenched her hands to keep from fidgeting. "He showed up at my cottage last night. I've never met or talked to him before then."

"Why did he visit you?" Fox asked.

"To find out if I'd seen anything at Candace's house to help identify the killer."

They exchanged interested looks. "And how did you reply?"

"I gave him the same answer I gave you." Melissa took a sip of coffee and frowned at the bitterness.

"Did you confide your belief that Candace was your mother?" Black asked.

She chewed her lip. "Yes."

"How did he react?"

She sighed and rubbed her forehead, tension knotting her neck. "He denied that Candace had a child, then he warned me not to spread rumors."

The detective's expression remained unreadable, but questions rallied in her mind. What would Latone do if it were true? How far would he go to keep the truth from being revealed?

Black shuffled, stared at his boots, then back at her. "Miss Fagan, do you know a man named Larry Dormer?"

She glanced at him, then at Fox. "Yes, he's a private investigator. He lives in Atlanta."

"Did he give you the information about Candace being your mother?" Black asked.

"Yes. Why? What does he have to do with Candace's murder?"

Fox settled his foot on the edge of another chair, then leaned forward, bracing his elbow on his knee. "When was the last time you saw him?"

Melissa swallowed, struggling to remember. "About three weeks ago, right before I moved here." Worry mushroomed inside. "Why?"

The two men traded speculative looks, then Black spoke in a low tone. "Because he was found murdered last night. And it looks like he's been dead for about three weeks."

ROBERT LATONE LIT his cigar, poured himself a bourbon on the rocks and paced to the window of his study, the conversation with Melissa Fagan grating on his strained nerves.

If the Fagan woman exposed the past, she could destroy his life and his daughter's reputation.

He had built an empire for himself with money, power and contacts worldwide. His sole heir and the only person who'd ever mattered to him, Candace, was dead.

He could not lose anything else.

A low knock sounded on the polished mahogany door, then Edward Moor, his right-hand man and confidant, appeared. "Mr. Latone, the limousine is ready."

Robert downed the bourbon in one sip, grateful for

the quick buzz of alcohol to dull the pain. Today was Candace's funeral.

He didn't know if he could stand to watch them put his baby in the ground.

Not that he hadn't lost her years ago, but he'd always maintained hope that the chasm between them would one day close and her vacuous behavior toward him would change. That he would have his real daughter back.

Now that would never happen.

"Mr. Latone?" Edward's low voice permeated the haze, and Latone moved across the room, smashing the cigar into the ashtray.

"Are you going to tell me about the meeting with that Fagan woman?" Edward said as they settled into the ride to the church for the funeral service.

Latone grunted. "She could be trouble."

Edward crossed his suited legs. "Elaborate."

"She claims she didn't see anything to help the police at Candace's house the night of the murder."

"That's too bad." Edward laid a hand over Robert's for a brief conciliatory moment, the black onyx inscripted ring shining in the sunlight. "Obviously you want her killer caught and punished."

Robert nodded. That went without saying.

"So who is this woman, and how did she know Candace?"

Robert stared into his friend's eyes. The secrets that lay between them were many, the cost of betrayal high if exposed. His fury was so strong he could barely contain his temper, but he controlled himself in order to test Edward's reaction. "She claims she's Candace's daughter."

Edward coughed, shock riding over his ruddy features. "But we handled that problem long ago." His hand shook as he lifted it and wiped perspiration from his forehead. "And we covered our tracks."

Robert gripped Edward's collar, tightening it across his throat. "You were in charge of the details," he growled. "You obviously talked to someone or left something uncovered."

Edward yanked at Robert's hands, his eyes bulging. "I swear I didn't, Robert. I don't know how she got any information...."

"I don't care how," Robert snapped. "I want this problem to go away. She can't ruin everything we've worked for. I won't allow it."

Edward nodded, heaving for air as Robert released him. Robert leaned back against the seat, his heart pounding as the church slipped into view. Edward understood him.

He'd take care of Melissa Fagan.

Chapter Eight

Eric had showered and dressed, and was waiting for Melissa when she returned to the rehab center. The first thing he noticed was that she appeared pale and shaken. The second was that she headed in the opposite direction as if to avoid him.

What the hell had happened?

He fully expected her to have another patient after him, but she stopped and spoke to the older nurse, Helen, then strode toward the exit at a hurried pace. Eric cursed the fact that he couldn't walk and wheeled his chair across the facility, trying his damnedest to catch her. By the time he made it down the handicapped ramp, she'd reached her car.

"Melissa!"

She froze, then fumbled with her keys and opened the driver's side. He rolled toward her in double time, determined to find out what had upset her.

"Melissa, wait!" The engine rumbled to life, but he caught the door before it closed and she could switch gears. "Wait, what's wrong?"

She angled her face to look at him, and he saw tears glittering in her eyes. He gently brushed his hand across her cheek, and she fell forward against him, her body trembling.

"What happened?" he asked gruffly.

She sniffed and pressed a hand against his chest. "You shouldn't be near me."

He cupped her face in his hands and lifted her chin, forcing her to look into his eyes. "What are you talking about?"

"It's too dangerous, Eric, stay away from me," she cried. "Everyone's getting killed."

"Melissa, you aren't making sense. Tell me what happened."

Her lower lip wobbled. "The private investigator I hired to find my parents…he's dead."

Eric stifled a reaction. "When?"

"About three weeks ago." Her voice quavered. "Right after I left Atlanta."

Her hands clutched his, panic straining her features. "The police think I had something to do with it. Don't you see? That's why they were here today, to ask me when I last saw him."

"They can't believe you murdered the man," Eric said. Surely the cops were smarter than that. "You have no motive." Unless she'd wanted to cover her tracks. If she'd set out to kill Candace, which he didn't believe.

She shrugged, her hands tightening on his arms. "I'm not sure they're convinced of that. And even if they don't think I killed Mr. Dormer, he might have been murdered because of the information he provided me regarding my parents."

That theory made more sense. But why would

someone go to such extremes to kill the private investigator?

Unless the killer thought the investigator knew more than he had told Melissa. But what exactly was the person hiding?

And if the private investigator's death was related to the Latone woman's murder and Melissa's investigation into her parentage, would she be next?

MELISSA PULLED AWAY, composing herself. "Eric, I have to go. Thanks for listening, but you have to stay away from me. I don't want you hurt."

"I can take care of myself," Eric said between clenched teeth.

Her gaze fell to the wheelchair. It stood between them, a visible reminder that he was physically debilitated and needed therapy.

He dropped his hands. "You don't have to be alone anymore, Melissa."

Fear rippled through her, along with memories of her past. Wanting someone to help but having nowhere to turn. Running from one of her foster fathers. Being locked in a closet by another. But acceptance of her childhood had made her stronger. She wouldn't surrender to the fear now. "Yes, I have to be alone." She laid her palm against his cheek, a surge of warmth seeping through her, replacing the icy chill in her bones. "I appreciate your concern, but I'd never forgive myself if something happened to you, Eric." *Because I might be falling in love with you.*

No, she couldn't be in love.

She was attracted to Eric, but there was too much

chaos in her life for her to entertain feelings for this man. After everything he'd endured the past few months, he didn't deserve someone with ready-made problems.

Besides, she knew nothing about relationships. Nothing except saying goodbye.

And now, because of her search for her parents, her love might be fatal.

"I need to leave, Eric."

"Where are you going?"

She hesitated. This morning she hadn't decided whether or not to attend Candace's funeral. With the realization that Candace and the P.I. had both lost their lives because of her search, she had to attend. She needed the truth or their deaths would count for nothing. "I'm going to Candace Latone's funeral."

Eric nodded. "Then let me ride with you."

"No."

He clutched her hand. "You're not going alone. If I don't ride with you, I'll call a taxi and come by myself."

"But why? It might be dangerous."

"Shh." He kissed her hand. "Because I don't want you hurt, either."

Melissa swallowed, emotions welling in her throat. No one had ever said those words to her before.

Why would this man who'd barely survived a terrible explosion put his life on the line for her, when no one else, not even her own mother or father, had wanted her?

GUILT NAGGED AT ERIC as he rode with Melissa to the funeral. It was ironic. His entire life, he'd helped other

women escape horrible family lives, yet this woman
was trying to protect him, when he should be the protector.

Devlin's words reverberated in his brain. *Use her to
get close to Hughes.*

He didn't like using people, especially innocent
women. And Melissa was about as innocent as they
came. Kind, caring, honest, compassionate. Alone.

All she'd wanted was to find the woman who'd
given her birth and to understand why she'd been
abandoned.

She knew nothing about Hughes, he was certain of
it.

But unfortunately, she had walked into a bed of lies
and danger she was not equipped to handle.

He cut his gaze toward her. Uncertainty plagued her
features as she parked in front of the Savannah church.
On the ride over, she'd stopped at a florist shop and
bought a bouquet of fresh flowers. A goodbye offering
for a woman she'd never met, a person who'd left her
as a baby to fend for herself in the world.

Yet Melissa still cared about Candace, which
proved she was a loving, forgiving woman.

Several cars lined the church parking lot, although
it was by no means full, a sad testament to the life of
the lady who lay inside in a casket ready to bid her
final goodbye. Seconds later, more cars rolled in, all
expensive makes and models. Affluent people
emerged dressed in black, obviously friends of Robert
Latone's who'd come to pay their respects and possibly win his favor. Eric wondered if any of them ac-

If offer card is missing write to: The Harlequin Reader Service, 3010 Walden Ave., P.O. Box 1867, Buffalo, NY 14240-1867

NO POSTAGE
NECESSARY
IF MAILED
IN THE
UNITED STATES

BUSINESS REPLY MAIL

FIRST-CLASS MAIL   PERMIT NO. 717-003   BUFFALO, NY

POSTAGE WILL BE PAID BY ADDRESSEE

HARLEQUIN READER SERVICE
3010 WALDEN AVE
PO BOX 1867
BUFFALO NY 14240-9952

Do You Have the LUCKY KEY?

PLAY THE Lucky Key Game

and you can get

FREE BOOKS
and a FREE GIFT!

Scratch the gold areas with a coin. Then check below to see the books and gift you can get!

YES! I have scratched off the gold areas. Please send me the **2 FREE BOOKS** and **GIFT** for which I qualify. I understand I am under no obligation to purchase any books, as explained on the back of this card.

382 HDL DVGA   **182 HDL DVGQ**

FIRST NAME   LAST NAME

ADDRESS

APT.#   CITY

STATE/PROV.   ZIP/POSTAL CODE

2 free books plus a free gift   1 free book

2 free books   Try Again!

Offer limited to one per household and not valid to current Harlequin Intrigue® subscribers. All orders subject to approval. Credit or Debit balances in a customer's account(s) may be offset by any other outstanding balance owed by or to the customer.

Visit us online at www.eHarlequin.com

tually cared about the woman inside, then realized he was projecting his feelings about his own mother's death on the visitors, and remembering the near-empty church where they had held her service.

A service his own father had not attended.

Only Cain had stood beside him, fending off the concerned social worker and assuming the role of a father figure to Eric. He'd have to thank his brother the next time he talked to him. Eric had never appreciated how much Cain had sacrificed to take care of him. He'd been angry, hurt, confused—not an easy kid to parent.

But nobody had cared for Melissa.

He would be there for her now.

Eric placed a hand over hers, the flicker of heat igniting between them. "Are you sure you want to do this?"

She nodded and curled her fingers into his, her voice stronger now. "Yes, Eric. I have to learn the truth."

God, he felt for her. "Robert Latone will be here."

"I know." She squeezed his hand. "And I doubt he'll be very happy to see me."

Probably an understatement. "But you don't intend to let Latone intimidate you?"

"Whether Candace was my mother or not, I feel connected to her, Eric. There had to be a reason I was the one who discovered her body that night."

Eric remembered his father's abusive behavior. The unfairness of it all. "Sometimes there are no reasons, Melissa. Things just happen. People are in the wrong place at the wrong time."

"I still have to finish this." Melissa released his

hand and closed her fingers around the flowers. "I have to know if Candace was my mother and if she died because of me."

"You think Robert Latone might have lied to you?"

"Maybe Candace never told him about the pregnancy. She could have hidden it, convinced a friend to drop me off at that church."

"That's true." He'd have to investigate the possibility. "But if he did know, and he's lying?"

"Then he might have forced Candace to give me away. Maybe exposing the truth will lead to Candace's killer."

Eric silently cursed as she exited the car. Melissa had raised some very good points. Whether or not this situation or her birth led to Arnold Hughes, he couldn't allow her to face Latone alone.

Because if she was right, and Latone was covering up his daughter's murder, then he would have no problem killing Melissa and covering up hers, as well.

MELISSA SLIPPED INTO the back of the church as quietly as possible, well aware Eric's chair squeaked slightly on the thick plush carpet. A hum of low whispers and greetings echoed from the pews as the visitors filled the rows, all well-dressed regal-looking men and women who were obviously friends of Robert Latone's. Had any of them been close to her mother, or even friends with her at all?

Robert Latone stood ramrod straight in the front row, shaking hands with a preacher clothed in a long robe. Melissa shivered, remembering the few times she'd attended church as a child. Her third foster father had been a self-proclaimed minister who preached hellfire and damnation and handled snakes. The experience had given her nightmares.

Later, as a college student, she'd visited the small chapel on campus and had felt solace in the quiet ceremonies and the softly spoken rituals of the Methodist congregation. Neither had compared to this ornate church with its stained-glass windows, carvings and decorative ten-foot ceilings.

Her gaze landed on the closed casket at the front of the church, pewter gray with a blanket of red roses. Red roses meant love—did Robert Latone really love his daughter?

The flower arrangement she'd bought seemed puny, but she still wanted to offer it as a gesture of…of what? Love, respect? She had neither for the woman. Only a deep sadness and curiosity, and regret that she'd died, even pity that Candace had missed out on a relationship with her own daughter—if she had wanted one. Had she?

The preacher moved to the pulpit, an organist accompanied another woman singing "Amazing Grace." Melissa slid into the last pew, her stomach churning. Eric moved up beside her and collected her hands in his.

"Friends and family, we are here today to say a final farewell to one of our sisters, a kind woman who lived alone most of her life, who gave to her small community of friends and rarely bothered others. Candace saw life through an artist's eyes, using various venues to portray her inner emotions and views of the world surrounding her." The preacher's words about living alone could have described *her,* Melissa thought, wondering if she and Candace shared anything else in common. Melissa certainly wasn't artistic.

The next few minutes passed in a blur while the preacher read scripture from the Bible, then recited a eulogy that sounded practiced and aimed toward helping Robert Latone accept his daughter's rise into the kingdom of heaven. Another hymn ended the short unemotional service.

Melissa studied Candace's father, her gaze straying to the gray-haired gentleman sitting next to him. She'd seen him before but couldn't quite place where. She also recognized the old man who'd given her directions to Candace's cottage and a few of the neighbors who'd arrived on the scene after the murder.

Robert Latone bowed his head and pinched his fingers to the bridge of his nose, his face stoic as the service ended, but his eyes remained dry. The other man led him through the procession to the side door and the guests followed accordingly.

There had been no open casket, no final moment for Melissa to speak to the woman she believed had given her birth. She wondered if Robert Latone had arranged a private viewing earlier between himself and his daughter. According to the local paper, he'd opted to forgo a traditional wake.

Melissa and Eric exited through the back, then fell into step behind the people moving to the graveyard behind the church, a well-tended manicured cemetery on the top of a hill. The sharp incline compounded Eric's wheelchair maneuvers, and she reached for the chair back to help him, but his fierce look dared her to insult him by offering her assistance.

At the graveside service, Melissa hovered in the throng of spectators while Robert Latone sat beneath the tarp that protected him from the late-afternoon sunshine. Odd, there was no other family present. Robert Latone might be a foreign diplomat and business tycoon, but either he had no other family or he'd distanced himself from them.

Had he been close to Candace throughout the years?

A breeze stirred and rattled the surrounding trees, scenting the air with the sweetness of the fresh flower arrangements the attendants were placing around the burial plot. Another Bible reading and prayer followed, then guests lined up to offer condolences. Melissa hung back. Latone's companion stared at her as if she'd invaded a private family gathering.

Finally, the crowd dispersed, the funeral staff began to shovel dirt onto the grave and Melissa forced her feet to move forward. Her heart aching that she'd been denied the opportunity to meet her mother, she knelt, whispered a silent goodbye and placed the flowers next to the grave.

Robert Latone's voice jerked her from her melancholy mood. "What are you doing here?"

She stood and faced him. "I came to pay my respects just like everyone else."

"You have no reason to be here."

Melissa gestured toward the parting crowd. "And all these people were her friends?"

He glared at her. "That's none of your business."

"Is there a problem, sir?" The gray-haired man who'd dogged Robert Latone all day approached her.

"No, Edward, I was just informing Miss Fagan that she doesn't belong here."

"He's right," the other man said. "This service is for friends and family only."

Melissa gave a sardonic laugh at his pointed remark. "And you don't think I'm family?"

"You're not," Robert Latone said.

"I have information which says otherwise," Melissa said.

"It's false information," Latone's watchdog said in a clipped voice. "Miss Latone never had children."

"And if she did, would you have recognized them?" Melissa asked, anger fueling her temper. "Or would you have forced her to get rid of her child so she wouldn't disgrace your reputation?"

Robert Latone's hand rose as if he might slap her. Eric's chair crunched gravel as he moved closer.

Edward's look turned lethal. "You should go now, Miss Fagan. Mr. Latone needs to grieve in peace."

Melissa shrugged his hand away. "I will find out the truth, Mr. Latone. No matter how much you attempt to hide it, secrets always have a way of coming out in the end."

Latone reached for her, but she strode away, her shoes kicking pebbles in her wake as Eric wheeled behind her.

Chapter Nine

After she dropped Eric off at his cottage, Melissa's chest ached with emotion. She opened the car windows and drove along the island, inhaling the salty air and pungent smell of shrimp and the sea, willing away the feeling of doom. She had always been alone—nothing really had changed today.

Yet it had.

All her life, she'd thrived on the belief that one day she'd be reunited with her mother. Now, that hope had been buried with Candace Latone.

She parked at a low-hung cliff at the corner tip of Skidaway, climbed down the hill and walked along the shore, taking solace in the soft sand beneath her feet and the crunch of shells as she walked. The tides rolled and crashed against the rocks, mimicking her tumultuous feelings over lost chances and dreams. Wrapping her arms around herself, she faced the ocean, marveling at the vast expanse of the endless sea and finally giving in to the pain swelling inside her.

If she disappeared into the water, no one would ever know…no one would miss her or care. She was like a broken seashell that would be lost in the vastness forever.

She sucked in a harsh breath at the realization, remembering all the times she'd felt hopeless as a child. All the times she'd reminded herself to hold on, that one day her parents might find her. That they loved her and wanted her.

She no longer maintained that belief. Robert Latone had completely denied her relationship to Candace or him and wanted nothing to do with her.

Kicking off her shoes, she walked toward the edge of the ocean, the water lapping over her feet and washing back out to sea. White billowy clouds rolled above her in a clear blue sky. Suddenly an image of Eric's face floated unbidden to her mind.

He had been like a rock to her all day, sitting silently and offering support, hovering in the background as if he understood that she needed space and time alone, but also suggesting that he wanted to protect her.

She was in love with him.

She had no idea how to handle these new feelings. There was already so much turmoil in her life that she desperately wanted Eric to hold her, to comfort her, to kiss her again and make her forget the sorrows of the day.

But she was on her own.

Or maybe she wasn't. Maybe she should talk to Eric.

He could go with her to the island, talk to Candace's neighbors. She really didn't want to go back to the island alone.

ERIC HAD BEEN SO FURIOUS with Robert Latone that he'd barely contained his rage. The fact that his physical limitations might prevent him from protecting Melissa had angered him even more.

But Melissa didn't deserve his wrath, not when her mother had just been buried and her grandfather had totally denied her existence. Did Robert Latone really think Candace hadn't given birth to a child, or was he trying to protect himself by covering up the fact that they'd both abandoned a baby? Was he worried about his reputation? His financial empire? Or some deeper secret being revealed?

Did he know the identity of the man who'd fathered Melissa?

Determined to unravel the truth, Eric spent the afternoon on the case. He needed fingerprints and DNA samples from the men he suspected might be Hughes. It would be tricky to obtain them without revealing himself though.

First, he paid a visit to Ian Hall, the new CEO of CIRP. Although the photo he'd discovered at Candace's suggested the improbability that Hall was Hughes, Eric had to make certain.

"I wanted to shake your hand and tell you how impressed I am with your center," Eric said.

"Thank you, Mr. Collier. We're proud of the facility and our staff." Hall's right eye twitched slightly as if he had a nervous tic. "I trust our staff is meeting your needs."

"Absolutely."

"You came here for physical therapy?" Hall asked.

"Yes, but I'm also scheduled for skin grafts. I needed time to heal first."

Hall nodded. "Our plastic surgeon, Crane, is top-notch."

"Yes, I've heard." He had given Clayton Fox a new face to fit his fake identity. Had he operated on Hughes, as well?

Eric glanced around the office, searching for a stray hair that might have fallen from Hall's jacket but saw none. He spotted the man's handkerchief and decided the Feds might be able to lift DNA from it.

Pretending interest in the diagram of the facility on the wall, he maneuvered his chair toward the desk. Hall followed, growing slightly agitated. "Do you have an interest in the center for some specific reason? Investment purposes maybe?"

"Perhaps."

"What exactly do you do, Mr. Collier?"

"I own a ranch in the North Georgia mountains. I'm planning a school for troubled teens and was curious about your counseling program. Perhaps I could talk to someone in the psychiatric department for a reference."

"Certainly." He scribbled a name on a business card and handed it to Eric. "Dennis Hopkins is phenomenal. He could definitely make some recommendations."

Eric intentionally dropped the card. While Hall bent to retrieve it, he swiped the handkerchief and stuffed it in his pocket.

"Thanks, Dr. Hall, you've been very helpful."

Hall followed him out, locking the door behind him. Eric wheeled back to his cottage and placed the card and handkerchief in a plastic bag to give to the authorities. He only hoped it provided them with some answers.

One more meeting with Dennis Hopkins. Maybe he'd surprise the man and show up unannounced. After all, if Hughes was hiding something, Eric didn't want to give him a chance to cover it up.

But as he stepped outside, he saw Melissa coming toward him.

"DR. HOPKINS, ARE YOU READY to begin with the patient?"

Hopkins glanced up from the file and nodded at the young nurse. So far, she'd expressed no personal interest in him, but that would change. If she didn't come around on her own, he'd have to do something. He'd wanted her the moment he laid eyes on her. Long auburn hair. Brown eyes. She was voluptuous, in spite of the fact that she camouflaged herself in those baggy uniforms. He wondered what she'd look like in an evening gown. Or naked.

"Dr. Hopkins?"

Damn. He wanted to play out the fantasy. "Give me five minutes. Go ahead and prep him."

"I think you may need to talk to him first. He's awfully agitated." She folded her hands across the clipboard, which she had nudged beneath her breasts.

Didn't she realize the movement only drew attention to her figure?

"All right. Go ahead and give him a dose of phenobarbital to calm him and I'll be right in."

She nodded, that mask of professionalism in place. He needed to work out how to push her romantic buttons. And if she rebuked him or didn't answer his needs, he'd turn her into putty in his hands.

He hurriedly skimmed the file, but the phone rang just as he stood. "Dr. Hopkins."

"Hopkins, listen, we've got trouble."

A curse word flew from his mouth. "What kind of trouble?"

"Someone's trying to hack into confidential files. The death of Robert Latone's daughter has drawn attention to the center. We can't let anyone find out what happened years ago."

It was always about protecting the past while he wanted to focus on the future. "Right."

"That new physical therapist, Melissa Fagan, the woman who found Candace's body, claims she's her daughter."

"Problematic."

"Word is that there may be a cop working undercover at the center, too."

"You think it's the Fagan woman?"

"We don't know yet. It could be another employee, hell, a janitor even. Or a patient. Keep your eyes and ears peeled."

"I will."

"And one more thing, hone up on those techniques. We may need to use them."

Hopkins grinned and thought of the unsuspecting guinea pig waiting in the other room. "Don't worry, I'm on it." He hung up and hurried toward the lab. The poor guy had no idea how the procedure would change him. Free will? Not with the new experimental drug, hypnosis and a little shock treatment.

Hell, the man would never know what happened. And if he didn't respond according to plan, he was dispensable, just like those three prisoners who'd traded early release time for their experimental services with that memory-altering drug. They were pawns in a very complicated, sophisticated, worldwide game of scientific chess.

A game Hopkins intended to win.

"WHAT KIND OF GAME are you playing, lady?"

Melissa fought to keep her voice level and smiled at the older storekeeper, grateful Eric had agreed to accompany her to the island. Just having him waiting in the car made her feel safer. "I'm not playing games, Mr. Wilks. And I didn't hurt Candace Latone." She prayed he'd see her sincerity. "I simply wanted to talk to her, but she was dead when I arrived."

He smacked his dentures. "You didn't have an insurance check for her?"

Melissa hesitated, debating whether the truth would gain his compassion or incriminate her more. "No, I'm searching for my mother. I was born in Savannah and was given information that lead me here, to Candace Latone."

His expression softened slightly, then suspicion registered as if he realized the implications. "You were upset 'cause she gave you away?"

"No." She bit her lip. "Well, of course, I had mixed feelings, but I didn't come here to do her harm.

You have to believe me, I simply wanted to meet her, to see if we had a chance at a relationship.''

He fumbled with a stack of newspapers, shifting them as if he needed something to do. ''You didn't ask her?''

''No.'' Melissa massaged her neck, the day's tension wearing on her. ''I wish I'd had the chance. Now I'll never know.''

He stared at her long and hard, then finally suggested, ''You might want to talk to Louise Philigreen. She and Candace were friends. Candace kept mostly to herself, but Louise liked art and gardening so they visited sometimes.''

Melissa thanked him and scribbled the directions, then hurried to the car. ''I found a friend of Candace's,'' she said. ''Maybe she can tell me something.''

''I hope you find what you're looking for, Melissa.''

She squeezed his hand, wondering why he looked so troubled. Five minutes later, she found the house. The spindly little fiftyish woman wore a big floppy sun hat and loose-fitting shift with tennis shoes and was watering her flower garden.

Melissa parked on the curb and climbed out. ''Mrs. Philigreen?''

''Yes?'' Louise smiled in welcome. ''Samantha?''

Melissa frowned. ''No, Ma'am, my name is Melissa Fagan.''

''Oh…oh, dear.'' She raised the brim of her hat and squinted. ''For a second there, I thought…well, never mind. What can I do for you?''

''Can we talk a few minutes?''

"Sure, hon, I love company. Samantha usually comes every day to visit. I don't know where she's been today."

"She sounds like a wonderful friend."

"Yes, actually she's my daughter. Would you like some lemonade?"

"No, thanks." Melissa gestured toward the mixture of spring flowers. "You have a beautiful flower garden."

"Thank you, I love to piddle. But Candace, she's the one with the green thumb." She bent to turn off the sprinkler hose and Melissa did it for her. "This morning, she told me she's entering her roses in the garden club fair," Louise tittered. "I've encouraged her to enter her roses for years."

Melissa glanced back at Eric and frowned. "Did you say you talked to her this morning?"

"Why, yes." She pressed a hand to her cheek. "We had tea and this apple coffee cake that I bake sometimes. Would you like some, Samantha?" She noticed Eric. "Oh, and tell your young man to come in, too."

A blush heated Melissa's cheeks. Eric simply smiled at the woman, opened the door and maneuvered himself into his chair. Louise took Melissa by the arm and Eric followed. "I'm so glad you finally came. I've been looking for you all day."

Melissa's heart sank as they settled on the porch. "This may be a waste of time," she told Eric while Louise gathered refreshments.

"You never know," Eric said. "Maybe she can tell you something."

The woman tittered out, bringing cinnamon-raisin

bread that had been store bought, not homemade apple cake.

"I'm so sorry, dear, I don't know what happened to the cake." Louise's voice quavered with agitation. "I guess Candace finished it off this morning. Have you seen her paintings?"

"Yes, a few," Melissa said.

"They are wonderful, aren't they?" She poured cold water in a mug over a tea bag. "Careful, don't burn yourself now."

Melissa nodded and accepted the cup, then handed one to Eric. "Thanks. Can you tell me anything else about Candace?"

"Well..." Louise sat down, and crossed her thin ankles. "She likes tulips and roses, and—what is that other flower?"

Sympathy filled Melissa. The woman obviously suffered from dementia.

"Did she ever talk about having children?" Melissa asked, hoping for a lucid moment.

Louise thumped her spoon on her cup. "I believe she had a boy. No...no, that was Inez that lives next door." Her soft green eyes met Melissa's. "I'm sorry, hon, what did you say your name was? You look so much like the baby girl I lost when I was young."

Melissa's heart stopped for a minute; could this woman be her mother instead of Candace?

No. Louise was simply confused.

"How did you lose your little girl?" Melissa asked.

"Oh, dear me, she drowned. It was so awful. I miss her so much..."

Eric reached out and gathered the woman's hand in between his. "I'm so sorry."

Her gaze met Eric's, tears brimming over. "You are such a nice gentleman. Thank you for coming."

Melissa was touched by Eric's sensitivity. She patted Louise's hand and thanked her, then they left.

"She was a sweet lady," she said in the car. "I almost wish…"

"That she was your mother."

She nodded. "I think I'll go back and visit her anyway. She seems lonely."

Eric turned brooding eyes toward the window, and Melissa frowned. What had she said or done that had upset him?

Eric gripped the seat, wanting to reach out and touch Melissa. To comfort her and reassure her that one day she'd find her family. But how could he do that when he suspected Hughes might be her father? When he was supposed to be using her?

And that poor woman, Louise…seeing her had only made him wonder what his own mother might have looked like now if she had lived.

Melissa pulled up to his cabin, and he reached for his wheelchair. The fact that he needed it was a bitter reminder of why he had to finish the job.

Hughes had to pay.

He just hated that Melissa might be hurt in the process.

But he wasn't the only one Hughes had hurt. And he had to put a stop to it.

MELISSA LET ERIC out at his cabin and drove to hers, tension knotting her neck. Why had Eric grown so sullen?

Wearily, she dragged herself inside. No sooner had she closed the door when a knock sounded. Maybe it was Eric coming back. Maybe he'd open up and tell her what was wrong.

Instead of Eric though, the man who'd acted as Robert Latone's watchdog at the funeral stood at the door. "Miss Fagan, we need to talk."

Melissa pressed her mouth into a tight line. "What about?"

"About you."

"Mr...?"

"Moor. I'm Robert Latone's personal assistant."

"I see. Well, Mr. Moor, unless you have information regarding my mother, then we have nothing to say to one another."

"You're wrong about that. Mr. Latone has suffered enough the last few days." He shouldered his way inside, and Melissa gasped, panic needling her. "He doesn't need you making false accusations about being his granddaughter or slandering his daughter's name by insisting she gave birth to an illegitimate child. Let Candace rest in peace."

"I want her to rest," Melissa said. "But I also want her killer caught."

"Good, then let us handle things." His hand shifted to the inside of his suit jacket pocket. Melissa backed up. Did he have a gun?

He removed a checkbook instead. "How much will it take for you to leave town and drop this matter?"

IT WAS AFTER FIVE by the time Eric arrived at Hopkins's office. A bulky man with tribal tattoos snaking up and down his arms exited the doctor's office as Eric entered. The man's expression was blank, his entire demeanor strange. What kind of treatment had he come for?

"Can I help you?" a young blond nurse asked from the receptionist's desk.

"Yes, I need to talk to Dr. Hopkins."

"I'm sorry, but he can't see you today. Is this for a consultation?"

"Yes, I've been suffering post-traumatic stress disorder relating to my accident," Eric said by way of a cover.

Shouting echoed from down the hall. Eric turned in the direction of the sound, curious.

"That's one of Dr. Hopkins's patients," she explained. "The poor man's psychotic, gets volatile at times." She sputtered a nervous laugh as the shouting grew louder, the patient's voice rising in hysteria.

"Listen, Mr. Collier, let me put you down for an appointment. I need to go help Dr. Hopkins."

"Sure." She squeezed him in for a brief consultation for the following week, and he wheeled toward the door, grateful she didn't wait for him to leave before she raced down the hall to assist with the patient.

Eric wheeled back in, opened the office door and scanned the room, searching for something that might offer Hopkins's DNA. He found a pen on the desk, dropped it in the bag he'd brought and slid it beneath him. At least he could get the man's prints. Eyeing the computer and the files on the desk, he noticed the initials GS–B-2, but the patient's voice grew quiet and he was afraid the nurse would return any minute.

Cursing the confines of his limited mobility, he wheeled out of the office and into the hallway. Outside, he breathed in the fresh air and glanced up at the building, wondering about Hopkins's therapy techniques. The research notes he'd read about earlier work mentioned special drugs being tested on patients, prisoners who'd traded early-release time to serve as guinea pigs. Had Hopkins continued the unethical procedures? What exactly did GS–B-2 stand for?

Anxious for the fingerprint results, as soon as he returned to his cottage, he phoned Detective Black. A half hour later, Black and Fox arrived to claim the items.

"We'll get them to Devlin," Black said. "Good work."

"I have a meeting with Dr. Hopkins next week, maybe I can find out more." He explained about the file. "I don't know what the initials GS–B2 mean, but it could be important."

"We'll check into it," Black said. "Have you learned anything from the Fagan woman?"

"She didn't kill Candace Latone."

"She tell you about the P.I.?" Fox asked.

"Yes, and I'm afraid Melissa's in danger."

Black and Fox exchanged concerned looks. "Be careful," Black warned.

"I can take care of myself," Eric grunted. "Robert Latone claims his daughter never had a child. We need to know if he's lying."

"We're on him," Black said. "And his hound dog, Edward Moor. The Feds have suspected Latone of espionage for years, but haven't pinpointed any concrete evidence.''

''Keep looking,'' Eric said.

''And you hang with the Fagan woman,'' Fox said. ''She might be our ticket to Hughes.''

Eric silently balked, although he knew they were right.

He still didn't have to like it.

They let themselves out, and he splashed cold water on his face, then grabbed his new cane. Maybe he'd visit Melissa tonight, and talk. After burying her mother today, she might need company.

Even if she said she wanted to be alone, he knew all about self-imposed exile. And he refused to allow her to give in to it.

''I THINK YOU'D BETTER leave.'' Melissa gestured toward the cottage door, livid.

Edward Moor settled his intimidating stare on Melissa's face. ''Don't be stupid, Miss Fagan. You have nothing to substantiate your claims. And I'm aware of your financial situation, you can use the money.''

''I'm not interested in your money,'' Melissa said. ''I came to Savannah for the truth, not to blackmail Mr. Latone.''

His eyebrow arch said otherwise. ''Mr. Latone would appreciate it if you left town. Soon.''

Melissa folded her arms across her chest. ''I can't do that.''

''You can't or you won't?''

''Both. In case you haven't read the papers, I discovered Candace's body, so that makes me a material witness in a crime. I've been told not to leave Savannah.''

"But you said you saw nothing."

"I didn't see anything, but the police still want me for questioning."

A sly grin lit his eyes. "Or they suspect you killed Candace out of revenge because you believe she abandoned you?"

"She did."

He scribbled an amount on the check, then shoved it toward Melissa. "Take this and keep your mouth shut. Or you might end up in jail for killing Candace. Mr. Latone would like to see the murderer caught."

Melissa glanced at the check and stifled a gasp. One million dollars.

If they intended to pay her that much, they definitely had something to hide. She accepted the check, then tore it into shreds, pushed the man out of the entryway and slammed the door in his face.

Furious and frustrated, she stripped off her clothes and climbed in the shower, wanting to wash away the ugliness of the day. Moor and his bribe repulsed her.

She needed to calm herself and sleep. Forget that he had darkened her door with the insinuation that she had sought out Candace for money, or that she would settle for a bribe in place of the truth.

How could Robert Latone care for that man and not his own grandchild?

Had he treated Candace in such a vile manner? If so, she could understand the woman falling for any man who offered the love her father had withheld from her.

She soaped herself and shampooed her hair, closing her eyes as the hot water beat a soothing pattern down her body. The soap bubbles slithered to the floor and swirled around her, the comforting task slowly washing away her anxiety. The soapy scent reminded her of Eric fresh from the shower after his therapy session, the scent triggering memories of his gentle comforting touches today and the kiss they'd shared.

She desperately wanted more. Wanted him to hold her tonight and erase the pain and emptiness of knowing that her hopes of having a mother had died with Candace. Images of Eric's large hands running over her body taunted her, and a titillating sensation stole through her body. What would it feel like for Eric to stroke her naked skin? To kiss and tease her in all those secret places that no other man had ever touched?

Wild sensations spiraled through her at the sheer thought. She turned off the water, toweled off and pulled on a terry-cloth robe. The soft fabric reminded her of the baby blanket one of her foster mothers had given her.

Another had taken it away, saying she was too old to cling to such nonsense.

If she ever had a child, she would never say such harsh things.

She dragged a brush through her long hair, combing out the tangles, then faced herself in the mirror and stared at her reflection. Why had her parents been unable to love her?

Why had anyone since?

She opened the medicine chest and reached for her medication, but a screeching sound startled her, and she hesitated to listen. The whisper of the wind? A tree branch scraping the window?

It sounded again, low and eerie. Her senses sprang to full alert, and she listened at the door. Nothing.

Still, caution interceded as she remembered the events of the past few days, and she slowly inched open the door, squinting through the dimly lit interior. Nothing. Certain her imagination was overreacting again, she stepped into the hall, but a large hand grabbed her around the waist, and another one settled over her mouth.

Melissa tried to scream, raised her leg to kick backward in a defensive move she'd learned when she was young, but her attacker knocked her in the head.

They both crumbled to the floor in a tangle of fists and fighting.

Chapter Ten

Melissa scrambled sideways, but the man's fist rammed into her chest, and she gasped. Pain sliced through her rib cage and cut off her oxygen. He flipped her to her stomach, jerked her arms behind her and twisted them upward, grinding her face into the floor. A needle jabbed her arm. Then the metallic taste of blood filled her mouth, and dizziness blurred her vision.

The phone trilled, over and over, and the message machine clicked on. "Hi, Melissa, it's Eric. I'm on my way. See you in a few minutes."

Tears dribbled down her face, the salty taste mingling with the blood as Eric's face flashed into her mind. She was losing consciousness.

And she had one last regret. She wished she'd made love to him before she died.

BEFORE ERIC COULD MAKE IT out the door, Cain called and then Luke Devlin.

"I talked to Black and received the fingerprints. Thanks, Collier."

"Tell me about this Dr. Hopkins."

"He's been working on hypnosis techniques with patients during therapy. Word is he might be involved in a special project for the government—GS–B2. Government-sanctioned brainwashing experiments.''

"Great. I'm supposed to see him next week.''

"Be careful,'' Devlin warned. "If he suspects the real reason you're there, you might end up a guinea pig.''

Eric's fingers tightened around the handset. Old distrust issues rose to haunt him. Eric had always seen the grays, never trusted anyone but his brother. Now he'd been forced to rely on Devlin and two local cops he'd met days ago. He didn't like it.

"What's happening with the Fagan woman?''

"She went to Candace Latone's funeral today. Latone wasn't happy to see her. He denied Candace had a child.'' He sighed and massaged a cramp in his upper thigh. "He's either in the dark about the baby Candace delivered or he's hiding something.''

"Interesting, considering his donations to CIRP. I've been doing some background research.''

"Anything new?''

"Apparently, doctors at the hospital ran a special fertility clinic back in the eighties. They were also researching a new birth control pill and experimenting with fertility drugs. Candace was in one of the experiments, but I'm not sure which.''

"Do you know who fathered her baby?''

"Everything points to Hughes. He had some kind of God complex, I guess. Figured his sperm was superior to others.'' A sardonic chuckle escaped him.

"Or maybe at that point in his career, he wasn't bold enough to involve outsiders in his experiments."

"Did he have a personal relationship with Candace?"

"It's too early to tell, but my sources believe he did. Even if he didn't, though, if Candace received the fertility treatments, Hughes was likely the father."

"Why would a single woman like her take fertility treatments?"

"To antagonize her father."

Eric let the comment stand. Had Candace gotten pregnant as a rebellious statement against Robert Latone? "An affair with Hughes would serve the same purpose and be even more personal. Get back at her daddy by screwing his friend."

"Right. Or maybe she was looking for a father figure and Hughes provided it."

"And he gladly took advantage of the fact." Eric's opinion of the man dropped ever lower on the scale of humanity. "God, I want to catch this bastard."

"I'm glad to hear you say that." Devlin paused. "You realize we finally have the perfect way to draw out Hughes."

Damn it. He was going to suggest Eric use Melissa as bait to trap Hughes. Eric did not want to tell Melissa her father was a monster, or lie to her and use her. "Hey, I want Hughes as bad as you do, but I refuse to put Melissa in the middle...."

"Think about it," Devlin said in a low voice. "We could finally arrest Hughes for all the lives he's hurt and still might hurt."

Eric remembered Cain and Alanna and little baby Simon. Hughes definitely posed a threat to his family.

What should he do?

MELISSA STIRRED, disoriented and gasping for air. She'd been bound and gagged and was trapped somewhere underground. The smell of damp earth assaulted her.

Where was she? A cave? A cellar? A basement? Was she still at CIRP?

The floor rocked beneath her, and for a moment she thought she was on a boat. Then the movement settled. The rocking motion was her own head spinning from the drugs. She dug downward with her elbows to lift herself but tasted dirt.

Fear snaked through her, claustrophobia mounting. Had her attacker buried her alive?

Panic stabbed at her, destroying rational thought. She struggled against the heavy ropes. Skin scraped and blood trickled down her hands. She didn't care. She had to free herself. Claw her way out of this hellhole. Scream for help.

Where was Eric? Was he close by? Had he returned in time to see the man who'd assaulted her drag her off?

The cloying odor of rotting foliage and a dead animal permeated her nostrils. She bit the inside of her cheek, nausea rising. A dead mouse. A rat. If there was one, there would be others. All sorts of bugs and creatures lived underground, ready to feed off her.

Stop panicking. Breathe slowly so you don't waste oxygen.

She tried to scoot downward to acclimate herself. The area was tight, only a few feet, like a basement crawl space. She rolled to her back, fighting the pain from her bruised ribs, but dizziness swept over her again.

A sob escaped, and she twisted onto her side, rocking herself back and forth. Terror overcame her. No one would ever find her here.

If only she'd taken a chance on Eric, if only she'd told him how she felt…but now he would never know. And she would die alone just as she'd lived all her life.

ERIC PROPPED THE CANE on his lap and wheeled along the path that paralleled the ocean, hoping the fresh salty air would clear his head. He desperately wanted to see Melissa tonight, but his need for her company had nothing to do with the case.

He did not want to use her or confess his suspicions about her father. She had received a devastating blow in finding her mother dead, and then having her grandfather deny her existence. How would she react if she learned she might be the daughter of a mad scientist who had killed innocent people and tried to shape others' lives with his twisted research and need for power?

The waves crashed against the rocks, a seagull swooped low on the sandy shore below to search for crumbs. A lone fisherman stood casting out his line. A patient, most likely. Eric had enjoyed fishing on the lake back home. When he'd invented the story about building a ranch for troubled teens, he'd realized it wasn't a bad idea. Maybe when he finished this mission, he'd draw up a plan. What would Melissa think of the idea?

The lake on his property could provide fishing for the kids and other recreational activities, the horses would offer the opportunity to ride, as well as work for the boys, and the on-site counselors would guide them back on track.

His emotions calmer, he headed toward Melissa's cabin. Tonight he would simply talk to her, offer her a shoulder if she needed one. Tomorrow he'd figure out a way to draw out Hughes without Melissa's involvement.

He wheeled across the quadrangle that separated the patient housing from employee cottages, frowning when he noticed her door ajar. Remembering the earlier break-in, he approached with caution. His pulse accelerated when he rolled inside the doorway and spotted a lamp shattered on the floor. Magazines had been scattered, and the coffee table sat sideways as if it had been kicked or moved. A damp towel lay on the carpet near the bathroom in a puddle. All signs of a scuffle.

"Melissa?" An eerie silence pervaded the room. "Melissa?"

No answer.

The first strains of panic wove through his system as he wheeled through the rest of the cottage. No Melissa. He raced back to the living area and scanned the room for any indication of where she might be. Her purse mocked him from the kitchen counter. Her car had been parked outside. She hadn't driven anywhere.

And judging from the strewn items on the floor, she hadn't left willingly.

Had Hughes discovered her identity and kidnapped her? Had Latone or one of his cronies decided to stop her from asking questions?

Had the killer who'd murdered Candace attacked Melissa?

He reached for the phone, his pulse pounding. Damn it, the line had been cut.

He slammed it down and raced outside. Thank God he'd brought his cell phone. He called the locals.

"We're on our way," Fox said.

Eric hung up, his fear intensifying, his frustration mounting. He had to do something.

Minutes could cost Melissa her life.

A noise rattled the brush. Footsteps maybe? He paused and listened. Nothing.

The wind howled off the ocean, the onset of a spring storm brewing in the distance. The temperature had dropped with the cloud cover, adding a chill to the air. Could Melissa have escaped her attacker? If so, she might be outside, running for her life. Where would she go? To him? Down to the water?

He scanned the pavement for footprints, anything to indicate where her attacker might have taken her, and noticed the grass had been flattened to the right. Something had been dragged over it.

A body maybe.

Praying he wasn't too late, he steered off the paved path onto the grassy area and followed the indented grass blades. Footprints that looked as if they'd been made by running shoes marred the dry ground, and a few fibers—terry cloth maybe? a bathrobe?—dotted the grass.

He wheeled faster, searching the area for someplace the perpetrator might have taken Melissa. Another patch of land next to one of the storage buildings that looked recently disturbed. Was she inside the building? He wheeled closer and checked the door, but it was padlocked from the outside. No windows. Damn.

He rolled around the outside perimeter, listening for signs of someone trapped inside, but heard nothing.

He contemplated giving up, when he noticed a small patch of land covering a storage door that led to a crawl space. Had the center built an underground shelter in case of a nuclear attack or some kind of chemical or biological spillover from Nighthawk Island?

He paused and listened. The wind howled again, but below its whine, he detected another sound. Scratching beneath the ground. A few white fibers lay in the grass nearby. Could Melissa be down in that hole?

Was she alive? Hurt?

He cursed his legs as he fought to free himself from the chair. Finally he managed to support himself with the cane and took two steps toward the covering. Slowly lowering himself, he crawled the rest of the way, then lay on his belly and pulled at the circular concrete covering. His muscles strained as he moved it aside. Darkness filled the mouth of the opening, a rancid smell escaping.

"Melissa?" He leaned farther into the opening and yelled her name again. "Melissa, are you there?"

Nothing.

"Melissa?" He leaned farther into the hole, searching for light, walls, anything to orient him. A scratching sound rose from the depths of the darkness.

Bracing himself on his hands and knees, he swung his body around and slid himself down into the opening, clawing at the sides and steps built into the wall. Using his upper body to support most of his weight, he moved down the steps, his weakened legs trembling as he descended. He half dragged himself the rest of the way. His hands dug at the dirt walls. His fingers bled from the jagged rocks he met on the way. Finally, he dropped to the floor and scrambled through the darkness toward the sound of the scratching. A sliver of light radiated from the mouth of the tunnel. Then he saw a body.

''Melissa?''

She lay facedown, her arms bound behind her, a gag around her mouth. One foot twitched back and forth. Her toe was bloody where she'd been trying to scratch the ground.

At least she was alive.

Emotions clogged his throat as he slid on his belly the remaining few feet to her. The hole was obviously the end of a tunnel, maybe an emergency escape from the storage building. His hands shaking, he lifted her in his lap and turned her over. She was limp, her eyes glassy, her breathing so shallow it was barely audible. Pushing dirt-covered hair from her face, he untied the gag to make breathing easier, and checked her for injuries. Blood seeped from a gash on the back of her head and another on her forehead.

''Melissa, talk to me, honey, wake up and look at me.''

She lay motionless in his arms though, her body icy cold, sending another bout of fear through him. Had she been drugged?

He remembered her seizure disorder, grabbed his cell phone and punched in Fox's number.

"We're on the island now."

"I found her," Eric said in a gruff voice. "Get an ambulance, she's in trouble." He gave Fox directions to the building, then hung up and rocked Melissa back and forth to comfort her.

Chapter Eleven

"Shh, Melissa, be strong, baby, you have to be all right." A siren wailed close by and roared up to the cottage. Black appeared first, his head in the mouth of the opening.

"Collier?"

"Yeah, we're down here."

"How's she doing?"

"She's unconscious. I...her body's cold and clammy, eyes are dilated." He wiped her damp forehead with his palm.

"We'll get a crime team to check her place," Black called. "How the hell did you wind up in there?"

"I crawled down to find Melissa."

"It's a miracle you didn't kill yourself. Hold on, we'll have you out in a minute."

Damn it, Eric thought. If he had full function of his limbs, he'd already have rescued Melissa himself. "She has some kind of seizure disorder, Black. I think she takes regular medication, we'll need the name of the meds for the hospital."

Fox's voice echoed to him, "I'll look for it in the cottage. The ambulance is pulling in now."

The siren wailed closer. Seconds later, he heard Black directing the paramedics to the tunnel. One rescue worker descended the steps, then rushed over, knelt and took Melissa's vitals. He yelled them up to the other paramedic. "We need a stretcher board down here. We'll lift her out."

He glanced at Eric. "Are you all right, sir? Do you have injuries?"

"I'm fine, just take care of her." He felt helpless as he watched the men work to save Melissa. They secured her to the stretcher, and with Black's help lifted her through the opening. The first paramedic returned to assist him.

"I can hang on to a rope if you can haul me up," he said between clenched teeth.

The paramedic nodded, and Eric crawled over and grabbed the end of the rope. Thank God he'd continued to lift weights and maintain his upper-body strength. He needed it now more than ever.

By the time Black helped him up, he'd grabbed his cane, and hobbled over to Melissa, the paramedics had started an IV. Fox raced back from the cottage with a bottle of prescription pills and handed them to the paramedics. They called the E.R. for instructions.

"We're ready to transport her." The first paramedic turned to Eric. "We need to check you out, sir."

"I wasn't hurt tonight," Eric said, hating his obvious physical problems. "But I'm going with you."

The paramedics traded questioning looks with the detectives, then one of them nodded.

"We'll search the cottage for evidence of her attacker," Black said.

"You'd better find him," Eric growled as he allowed the paramedic to help him into the ambulance. "The SOB has to pay."

"Is our problem extinguished?"

"Not exactly." He scrubbed a hand over his sweating face, cursing aloud. "I planned to finish her off at her cottage, but that damn crippled guy called. He was on his way. I put her in the crawl space so I wouldn't get caught. I thought she'd suffocate there or I could go back later and complete the assignment, but Collier found her."

"Who is this Collier? What does he know?"

"I'm not sure. He's a patient, Melissa Fagan is his physical therapist."

"Hmm. Find out more on the man."

"Right."

"Do I need to take care of the Fagan problem myself?"

He rolled a cigarette between his fingers, yanked out a match, but decided to wait until the paramedics and cops left the vicinity before he lit up. "No, I can do it." He had been trained well. The mission was part of his initiation; he had to complete it, live up to the symbols tattooed on his arms. The scent of the kill taunted him. He could taste the blood, death.

And he knew exactly where to finish the job—at the hospital, right under all the unsuspecting noses.

MELISSA FELT AS IF she was drifting through a haze of never-ending darkness. She swam through the murky water, but the undertow dragged her deeper into the abyss, pulling at her legs and arms. Unknown terrors waited for her as she traveled deeper, a thick quicksand-like marsh sucking her underneath its muddy, brown folds. She couldn't see. She couldn't breathe.

She couldn't fight it.

After the pain, the darkness, there had to be a light. Peace. Freedom. She ached to find it.

''Pulse is weak and thready, she's not breathing! We're losing her!''

Voices echoed through the haze. Distant, far away. The droning of other noises interceded. A wailing sound like a siren. Then she was moving again, plowing through the water. Thick weeds and underbrush battered her body and gouged her skin like talons. Something hard slammed against her chest, and she bucked upward. A puff of air sifted through the concentrated quicksand, exploding into her mouth and lungs.

''Fight it, Melissa, fight it.''

Fingers yanked at her, trying to pull her back through the murkiness, but a whirlwind sucked her the other way. ''Come on, breathe, damn it!''

A coldness settled around her, chilling her to the bone. Numbness slowly seeped through her, obliterating the pain. She was floating. She welcomed the lifeless sensation, wanted to escape the suffocating darkness where she was all alone.

''Don't you dare give up, Melissa,'' the voice whispered. ''You're not alone. Do you hear me, you're not alone. I'm here.''

But she was alone. The floating felt so peaceful....

"Melissa, I care about you, please, don't give up. Come back to me."

She began to spin in circles, weaving through the darkness, around and around. The pain was back, pricking at her skin, the air thick with death, the light...

"I'm here, Melissa, hold my hand and fight." Her hand moved upward, pressed against something coarse, damp. A face, tears.

Eric. He was calling her name, dragging her from the well of darkness.

"I need you, Melissa. I've never said that to anyone but my brother, but I need you. Please don't leave me here alone."

The pain receded, faded to a dull droning ache. Light burst through the gray. A soft halo of someone's face.

Eric's.

She wiggled her fingers in an attempt to squeeze his hand, but she was so weak, she didn't know if he could feel it.

ERIC CRADLED MELISSA'S hand in his, pressing it against his cheek. He lowered his head, emotions battling to the surface. He couldn't lose her. A flutter of her fingers, and he jerked his head up.

"She's breathing on her own again," the paramedic said.

Relief surged through him.

He stroked her cheek. "Melissa, hang in there, you hear me. You're strong, you're going to be all right."

Her squeeze felt stronger this time, and he finally

released the breath he'd been holding. The ambulance barreled into the hospital parking lot, and the paramedics catapulted into motion, barking details of her condition to the doctors and nurses waiting to greet them.

The second paramedic helped Eric from the ambulance. His legs felt unsteady as the man assisted him in, and brought him a wheelchair. Now his adrenaline surge had petered off, the familiar ache of his injuries had returned.

But at least he had been able to save Melissa.

They rushed her into the E.R., and he wheeled into the waiting room, for the first time since his accident, craving the sweet relief of nicotine.

He felt so damn helpless.

Black and Fox were investigating Melissa's cabin for evidence and the doctors were taking care of Melissa. What the hell could he do but wait?

The familiar scents of the hospital bombarded him, reminding him of his long stint in the burn ward. Cain must have been out of his mind when he'd thought Eric had died in the explosion. His brother had thrown himself into saving Alanna and Simon as a favor to Eric, but thankfully, Cain had found love in the process. His brother deserved it.

He punched in Cain's number. Alanna answered on the third ring. "Hello."

"Alanna, it's Eric."

"Eric, we were just talking about you. How are things at CIRP?"

"That's why I'm calling. Can I speak to Cain?"

"Sure." She sounded worried but she called Cain to the phone. His brother cooed to baby Simon, then said hello.

"What's wrong, Eric? Are you in trouble?"

He explained about the incident with Melissa. "I don't want her to die," Eric admitted in a gruff voice. "And Devlin wants me to use Melissa to bait Hughes."

Cain hesitated. "You're falling for her, aren't you?"

Eric scrubbed a hand over his face. "I don't know. I...but I don't want anything bad to happen to her."

Cain chuckled. "You always were a sucker for a woman in trouble." Cain whispered something to Alanna. "Then again, I guess I should be grateful. I would never have met Alanna or Simon if you weren't such a good-hearted bastard."

"I'm not good-hearted," Eric growled.

Cain snorted in disbelief. "Do you want me to come to Savannah? Say the word, and I'm there."

"No. You need to stay with your family."

Family...the one thing they'd both lost early on.

"Do what you think is right," Cain said. "But be careful, Eric. And call me if you need me."

Eric hung up, feeling marginally better. He was glad Cain had a new family. But what about him? Did he deserve to have a woman in his life?

Or was he destined to live his life alone?

He glanced down at his scarred body. Would any woman be able to accept him the way he was now? Would Melissa...

He wanted to touch her, taste her, tell her the truth.

But she would hate him when she learned he had lied about his identity.

"Mr. Collier?"

Eric jerked his head up, shocked to find the CEO of CIRP, Ian Hall, standing in front of him. "What are you doing here?"

Hall dug his hands into the pockets of his suit pants. "I heard one of our employees was hurt and had to be admitted."

Eric bottled his volatile emotions. "*Hurt* isn't exactly the right word. Melissa Fagan was assaulted, bound and gagged and left to die in some underground crawl space next to one of the storage buildings."

"My God." A concerned frown creased the skin between Hall's eyes as he dropped into a chair beside Eric. "How is her condition?"

"I don't know. I'm waiting to hear now."

Hall raked a hand through his neatly clipped hair. "Do the police have any idea who attacked her or why?"

"The police are searching her cottage for evidence now."

"Was there a robbery?"

"No sign of one."

"I'll alert Seaside Security to watch for outsiders, beef up security and put a special guard on Miss Fagan's place."

"What if it wasn't an outsider?"

Hall's face blanched. "What are you suggesting, Mr. Collier?"

"That someone on the staff might be involved."

"That's ridiculous." Hall reached for his cell phone. "By the way, what exactly is your relationship to Miss Fagan?"

"She's my therapist," Eric said, refusing to elaborate.

A doctor approached then and Hall stood. Eric gripped the wheelchair arm. "How is she?"

"We've stabilized her for now. The drugs, coupled with the blow to the head, triggered a seizure, but she should be all right by tomorrow." He folded his hands in front of him. "We need to keep her overnight for observation."

Eric nodded. "Of course."

"Good work, Dr. Curry." Hall shook the middle-aged doctor's hand. "And please call me if there are any changes in her condition. I want to know immediately."

"I certainly will."

Hall turned, offered his hand and Eric accepted it. "I heard you made a pretty heroic rescue, Mr. Collier. As the director of CIRP, I want to extend my thanks. We value each of our employees and patients here." He dropped his hand. "And please let me know if you see something suspicious or if Miss Fagan has information about her attacker. I'm sure Seaside Security will do whatever it can to find the person and see justice served."

Eric watched Hall walk away. He had said all the right things, made all the right moves.

Was he on the level, or was he hiding something?

AN HOUR LATER, they had finally settled Melissa into a private room. Eric had phoned Black to relay her condition and to ask if they'd discovered anything. The police didn't have the results of the fingerprint tests, but they had bagged a stray hair, which they were testing for DNA.

Shanika, a kind African-American nurse, strode in, introduced herself and patted his arm. He figured he looked pathetic, all dirty and exhausted, parked beside Melissa's bed, but he didn't care.

"You can stay with her, but don't expect her to wake up before morning. She's weak and suffered a trauma." The nurse took Melissa's vitals and recorded them on her chart. "Fatigue also follows this type of seizure, along with a depressed mood. Both will fade, but she needs rest and time to recover."

Eric nodded. He was a patient man. He wasn't going anywhere. He'd give her all the time in the world to recover. In the meantime, he'd do his damnedest to keep her safe.

Shanika graced him with an understanding smile, then left the room. Eric wheeled closer to Melissa and cradled her hand in his, rubbing her fingers between his to warm her. The other hand was hooked to an IV, the constant drip a reminder that she'd nearly died earlier. Bruises marked her forehead, and a scrape on her cheek testified to the brutality of the crime.

He hated men who used physical force on women, and had vowed he would never raise his hand to a female or child.

But now he wanted to kill the bastard who'd hurt her.

Trying to tamp his anger, he kissed her fingers one by one, then pressed them against his cheek. Her eyelids fluttered. For a second, he thought he'd imagined it, but then they fluttered once more, opening partway. Her eyes seemed unfocused, and she blinked, as if searching through the haze of drugs and pain.

"I'm right here, Melissa, you're going to be all right."

A frown pulled at her mouth and she tried to speak, but no sound came out. She wrestled beneath the covers though, as if struggling with her assailant.

"Shh, don't talk now. Just rest." He stroked her hands again. "Tomorrow will be soon enough for you to tell me what happened. Tonight, rest, concentrate on getting better."

Her eyes fluttered again, then closed, and her breathing became more even, but her body jerked once more, a moan rumbling from deep within her.

Her anguish tore him in two, but he continued to hold her hand and to whisper nonsensical comforting words until she finally settled into a deep peaceful sleep.

DAMN IT, HE DIDN'T THINK that Collier guy was ever going to leave the woman's side. He must be some kind of desperate. Of course, after looking at the man, no doubt he'd be hot to trot for anything with two legs that smiled at him.

He checked his watch. Two-thirty. Finally the man wheeled his chair from the room and headed down the hall. But he still had to get rid of the security guard plastered to the woman's door.

He had a plan. Had been trained well for his mission.

Slipping down the hall and around the corner, he spied the storage room. Inside were the janitor's cleaning chemicals. With a gloved hand, he read the contents. Just as he thought. Volatile as hell.

Stifling a laugh, he sprinkled the chemicals on the cleaning rags, dumped them in a big garbage bin in the small room, then dropped a lit match into the center. The flame ignited, caught the chemicals and began smoldering,

Covering his face with a surgical mask to match his scrubs, he slipped out of the room before the smoke curled through the doorway. He moved down the hall unnoticed, then waited in the corridor across from his victim's room until a nurse noticed the string of smoke.

"Fire!" She waved her arms to attract someone's attention.

Another nurse ran up, someone shouted at the security guard, and the guard jogged down the hall to help.

He chuckled beneath the mask. So easy.

Flexing his hand beneath his lab coat, he reached inside for the hypodermic and slid soundlessly into Melissa Fagan's room. She was sleeping like a baby, already so exhausted from their earlier jaunt that she didn't even stir. Damn. It really was more fun when they put up a fight.

Still, he had to finish her off tonight.

He raised the needle, injected the drug into her IV, turned and walked from the room. She would be dead before morning. Before anyone discovered she'd been given the wrong combination of drugs.

And no one would ever know the real reason—or who had killed her.

Chapter Twelve

Eric had almost reached the elevator when the smoke alarm sounded. He'd intended to get some fresh air, then return and sit by Melissa's side for the night, but he spun the wheelchair around and raced back down the hall. No way could he leave Melissa if a fire had broken out. He searched the corridors, his suspicious nature surfacing. What better diversion for a personal attack on a patient than a fire?

Heart beating double time, he rounded the corner and nearly crashed into a young orderly.

"Sir, can't you hear the alarm? This isn't a drill, you have to evacuate now."

Eric shrugged off his concern. "I can't leave, not until I know my friend is okay."

"Look, buddy, it'll be hard enough to get patients out if we need to, much less the visitors, especially handicapped ones."

Fury balled in Eric's stomach. "Let me worry about myself. Now, take your hands off the chair, or I'll do it for you."

The young man jumped back, and Eric wheeled down the hallway toward Melissa's room, bypassing a doctor and nurse in earnest conversation, then a surgeon, who cut his eyes toward Eric, his steps clipped, his attention returning to the file in his hands.

The nurses' station was empty, the crew gathered down the hall near a storage closet where the fire had apparently broken out. He scanned the hallway by Melissa's room, but the security guard had left his post to check on the source of the fire.

Livid at the man's incompetency, Eric approached the hospital room. Fear for Melissa tightened his gut as he opened the door.

She lay still in the bed, her breathing a series of hard rasps. He glanced at the IV, remembered the surgeon rushing down the hall, and panic slammed into him.

He turned and called into the hallway, "Help, room 111! Emergency!"

Without waiting further, he ripped the IV from Melissa's arm and yelled for help again. Shanika rushed in, saw Melissa's agitated breathing and ran to the door.

"We need a crash cart stat!"

Eric cradled Melissa's hand. "Hang on, honey, help is on the way. Don't give up."

Seconds later, a team of nurses and doctors ran in, and Eric moved aside while they treated her. Once she resumed breathing, he was banned to the waiting room, so he phoned Detective Black and filled him in.

"I want one of your guys here," Eric said. "That Seaside Security guard left her alone."

"A rookie mistake," Black said.

"Yeah, one that almost cost Melissa her life." Eric

blew into his balled fist to release his pent-up frustration. "I don't trust CIRP's security. For all we know, Hughes, or whoever is involved in this conspiracy, has the security team in his pocket."

"You're probably right," Black said. "I'll assign someone immediately."

It galled Eric that he'd had to ask for help. He thanked Black and hung up, then rolled back to Melissa's room. He had almost lost her twice today.

He wouldn't let it happen again. He only hoped that when Melissa woke, she could tell them something concrete to lead them to her attacker.

MELISSA STIRRED FROM a troubled sleep, her body languid and heavy. She struggled to open her eyes, finally forcing them partway open, only to look through a foggy haze. Where was she? What had happened? Why did she feel so exhausted and drained and …confused?

Memories crashed back. The shower…someone had attacked her, she'd been tied and gagged and left in a cave to die. The claustrophobia—she couldn't breathe. She had to claw her way out. Then voices. Eric beside her. Lifting her, murmuring sweet loving words, whispering that she wasn't alone. The darkness, then the brilliant white light had beckoned her, but he had called her back.

Emotions welled inside her. Where was she now?

The whine of an IV drip and another sound—snoring—drifted through her consciousness. She twisted sideways. Eric's dark head lay facedown on the edge of her bed. His hands were curled around her free one, and he'd fallen asleep. He had stayed with her all night.

"Eric?" It hurt to talk, her mouth was so dry, like cotton.

He jerked his head up, the remnants of sleep and fatigue lining his handsome face.

Love for Eric swelled in her chest.

But what could she do about it? Someone was trying to kill her. She couldn't put him in danger.

If your father is trying to keep you from finding him, maybe you don't want to know who he is.

"Melissa, thank God, you're finally awake." Worry deepened his gruff voice.

"How…" She paused and wet her parched lips. "How long have I been here?"

"Since last night." A small smile tugged at his lips. "But it feels like days."

"You stayed all night?"

He nodded, lifted her hand and planted a kiss in her palm. "I promised you I wouldn't leave you alone."

"You always keep your promises?"

His eyes clouded. "I do my best."

She felt such a connection with him that it frightened her. What had she done to deserve his kindness? And how would he react if she confessed that she was falling in love with him?

"You should be at your place resting. And your therapy—"

"Don't worry about me, Melissa." He brushed her hair away from her forehead. "You need to take care of yourself."

She shrugged and angled her head down to study

their hands. The nightmare from the evening before flashed into her mind again. She'd had a seizure, she was certain of it. That accounted for part of her fatigue. She didn't want to be weak, to appear helpless in front of Eric.

"You rescued me?"

He released a self-deprecating laugh. "I had some help."

"But you climbed down in that hole to save me." Her gaze met his again. "Your legs?"

"They're fine," Eric said, denying the mutinous throbbing that had taken root in the wee hours of the morning.

"You need to stretch, go to the rehab center, have Helen work the muscles—"

"Shh." He pressed a finger to her lips. "I told you to stop worrying about me."

"Promise me you will, Eric. I don't want you to have a setback."

He didn't want that, either. He'd progressed too far. "All right, I promise."

A knock sounded at the door, then Detective Black poked his head in, and glanced from Melissa to Eric. "If it's all right, I'd like to ask you some questions, Miss Fagan."

She nodded, residual fear resurfacing. But she had to talk to the police sometime. She might as well get it over with.

ERIC FORCED HIMSELF to give Melissa some space while Black questioned her. Or maybe he needed space or he'd cling to her like a lovesick puppy.

Hearing the details of Melissa's ordeal only fueled his fury more. He stared out the window, watching each nurse and doctor who entered and exited the building, his distrust growing like a cold virus. Someone had disguised himself as a surgeon, slipped into Melissa's room and tried to kill her.

Was it someone who worked at CIRP? Robert Latone or one of his hired guns?

"Did you see the man's face?" Black asked.

"No." Melissa's voice was fading by the minute. "He grabbed me from behind. We struggled, I kicked him, but he hit me. I must have blacked out."

"And when you woke up?"

"I was tied, already in that…that hole."

"Did he say anything while he was attacking you? Did you recognize his voice?"

"No." She paused. "I…I remember the message machine clicking on…it was Eric saying he was coming over."

Black sighed. "He probably dragged you to the crawl space so Eric wouldn't catch him."

"Or he would have killed me then," Melissa said, echoing Eric's own thoughts.

Black gave a clipped nod.

"Eric saved my life." Melissa's voice dropped even lower.

Thank God, Eric thought. He'd catch the man who'd tried to kill her if it was the last thing he ever did.

MELISSA FINALLY PERSUADED Eric to rest, but he had only agreed after Detective Black had assigned one of his men to guard her door.

The next morning, when she was released, she felt like a prisoner in her cottage, the guard a visual reminder that someone had actually attempted to kill her.

After showering and dressing, she poured herself a cup of coffee. Should she forget her search and return to Atlanta? Two people had already died because of her, and she had almost lost her own life. If Eric hadn't rescued her…

She did not want him hurt because of her.

The letters she'd brought with her from Candace's house mocked her from her bedside table. Although she'd read them already, maybe she'd missed something that might clue her in to her father's identity.

Dear Baby,

I miss you so much. Every time I see a young mother pushing a stroller at the mall or running along the beach collecting seashells with their toddler, my heart squeezes into a gigantic knot. They say pain becomes more bearable as time passes, but each day I only miss you more.

Today, I painted an ocean scene and added a sand castle, one I wish we could build together. I imagine your face lit up with animation, your eyes bright with laughter. Your skin would be turning pink, so I coat you with sunscreen and tie a bonnet around your head to protect your delicate face.

I picture what you look like in my mind. You would be two years old today. Do you have my wiry hair and artistic eye? Or did you inherit your father's straight locks and detail-oriented mind?

Wherever you are, sweetheart, know that Mommy loves you. Maybe someday I'll get to hold you in my arms again.

Love,
Your mama

Melissa pressed the letter to her chest. Candace had loved her and wanted her. But she'd given her away and pined for her afterward.

Melissa could not return to Atlanta without knowing the truth about why she'd given her away or who had killed her.

Eric's face flashed into her mind. Tonight she'd tell him they couldn't see each other again.

She'd do anything to protect him.

IN SPITE OF LOSING a night's sleep, Eric felt surprisingly strong. Adrenaline surged through him as he worked through his therapy. Although he didn't enjoy the session with Helen near as much as he enjoyed working with Melissa, she seemed kind and allowed him to increase his routine.

"Are you sure you're ready to lose the chair?" Helen asked.

"Yes, ma'am. I'm tired of being confined." Besides, he'd taken steps with Melissa, then the night she was attacked.

"Don't overdo, Mr. Collier."

"I won't. Melissa warned me about a setback."

"Dear, I hope that girl's doing okay." Helen's forehead furrowed. "I can't believe someone assaulted her right on CIRP's property."

He wondered if Melissa had confided her reasons for being in Savannah to Helen. "You've worked here a long time, haven't you?"

Helen nodded. "When it was just a plain hospital with a few research labs."

"You knew Arnold Hughes?"

"Not personally." Helen shifted her plump body, looking uncomfortable with Eric's question. "Why all the interest in the center?"

"Curiosity. Too much time on my hands, I suppose, so I've been reading."

She nodded. "There's Mr. Stinson, let me get him started while you finish those reps."

"Sure." He pumped the weight with his leg, glancing sideways as she hurried to greet the war veteran. His craggy features looked tired and frustrated. Eric had never been a religious person, having lost his faith the day he and Cain had discovered his mother's suicide, but today he thanked the heavens the doctors had been able to save his legs.

He finished the weight lifting, then practiced walking with the support of the bars, increasing his speed and control daily. A session in the whirlpool relaxed his muscles later, then he showered and headed over to see Melissa. He allowed himself to use the chair on the way to her place, but he carried his cane.

Tonight he planned to walk in to see her and surprise her. He couldn't wait to see her face.

MELISSA RATIONALIZED her dismal mood as an after-effect of her seizure, but her quest for her parents and the recent attacks on her life complicated things more. And then there were her feelings for Eric, feelings she'd never had for another man…

She needed to take a long walk along the beach, to think and put her life in perspective, but she no longer felt free to do so. Danger lurked in every shadow and corner.

And walking with a guard didn't seem conducive to soul-searching.

A knock sounded at the door and she started, stuffing the last of Candace's letters into her bedside table. Assuming it was the officer stationed outside the cottage, she hurried to answer it, but found Eric on her doorstep.

"Hi."

She drank in his features, reminding herself she had to end this maddening flirtation, or whatever they were doing. "Hi."

"Can I come in?"

"Actually, I was going for a walk on the beach."

His dark eyebrow raised, and he glanced at the officer. "That sounds good. Let's go."

"But…"

"You're not going alone." Eric gestured toward the cop. "It's him or me."

No choice. "All right." She slipped on a wind-breaker, then stepped outside and began to follow the paved path to the shore. Eric followed, filling the silence with chitchat about his therapy session with Helen.

"She's been very nice to me," Melissa said. Barring the time she'd asked about the labor/delivery unit.

"It's easy to be nice to you, Melissa."

Her heart lurched. They'd reached the sand and she turned to Eric. It would be difficult to maneuver the chair down the beach. "I won't go far."

"I'm going with you."

She started to shake her head, but he pushed himself up, then gripped the cane and took a step toward her.

"Eric—"

"I'm improving," he said. "Not ready to jog yet, but I can manage a short walk."

Assuring herself it would be therapeutic for both of them, she allowed him to join her, but mentally gauged the distance. "You've made amazing progress, Eric."

"I have a great physical therapist."

His husky voice massaged her frayed nerve endings, igniting desire and other emotions she didn't want to deal with. They walked several feet in silence, the salty breeze lifting her hair, the scent of the ocean and sound of the waves crashing on the shore soothing her.

"It's really beautiful here," Melissa said. She sat down on the edge of a huge boulder to give Eric a rest, and stared out at the vast sea.

Eric leaned against the rock and nodded, but he wasn't looking at the ocean. His gaze warmed her face. "So are you."

Her breath caught when she turned and saw the hunger flaring in his eyes. Then, he raised his hand, slid it behind her neck and lowered his mouth to hers. She hesitated a fraction of a second, but the moment his lips dampened her own, she was lost in the sweet bliss of his caress.

ERIC COULDN'T HELP himself. Ever since he'd found Melissa unconscious in that damn hole, he'd wanted to hold her and kiss her. He had almost lost her twice, he needed reassurance that she was here, in his arms, alive.

She tasted like sweet berries and desire, a heady mixture that immediately sent a bolt of longing through him. He threaded his fingers into her silky hair, desperate to obliterate the image of her near death.

He wanted her. Ached to make her his.

A low moan escaped her lips, heightening his hunger even more. He teased her lips apart with his tongue and probed the warm recesses of her mouth, seeking, yearning, exploring, telling her silently how he wanted to love her. She clutched his arms, her breathing ragged as he lowered his mouth and kissed her neck, planting teasing tongue brushes all along her neck as his hands stroked her back, then moved to her waist. She groaned again and moved against him. He slid his hands beneath her jacket to cup the plump mounds of her breasts in his hands.

He wanted more.

She was fire in his hands, a literal flame that had caught, ready to burn out of control. He wanted to extinguish her desire by tearing off her clothes and thrusting himself inside her, but reined in his animalistic urges and slowed the pace to prolong the pleasure.

The wind whispered around them, the surf playing

a symphonic love song as he lifted his hands to her face. "Melissa, I...I want to make love to you."

Her passion-glazed eyes fixed on his face for a fraction of a second before reality intervened. That moment of hesitation cost him, he realized, but he couldn't regret giving her the choice.

"I...no, Eric, we can't do this."

"Why? Because I'm your patient."

She dropped her head forward. "Partly."

"Then Helen can continue my therapy."

Her gaze shot up to his. "No...there's more."

"You mean there's another man?"

She shook her head, obviously collecting her thoughts. "I...we can't. I mean, I like you, Eric, and you've been kind to me—"

"Kind?" His voice hardened. "I don't want your pity, Melissa."

She chewed on her bottom lip, and bolted to her feet. "I'm sorry, then, because that's all I have to give."

Eric jerked back, her words hitting him with more force than any physical punch could have caused. Then she turned and ran back up the beach, leaving him to hobble after her, with his heart in his throat.

ROBERT LATONE PEELED the end off the cigar wrapper, raked his hand through his clipped hair and frowned at the headlines as he read silently to himself.

Local Physical Therapist Attacked on CIRP Premises

Attacker unknown, but police are investigating the matter and hope to apprehend the assailant.

Ian Hall, CEO of CIRP, claims he is cooperating fully with the police and will provide extra security until the matter is solved.

The maid knocked on his office door. "Mr. Latone, two detectives are here to speak to you."

Robert barked a sarcastic laugh. What had taken them so long?

A broad-shouldered man with dark hair that needed trimming, and another brown-haired detective he recognized from the publicity about the failed memory transplant experiment, appeared.

The one called Black introduced them both. "Mr. Latone, we need to ask you some questions."

"Certainly, gentlemen." He gestured toward the leather wing chairs opposite his desk. "I hope you're here to tell me you've arrested the person responsible for my daughter's murder."

The detectives exchanged odd looks. "We're working on it," Black said.

"Actually, we need to ask you about Melissa Fagan."

Ah, he figured. "Yes, the young woman who found Candace's body. Does she have more information?"

"Not exactly. In fact—" Fox nodded toward the paper on Robert's desk "—you read that she was assaulted."

"Yes. Do you think this attack has something to do with Candace's murder?"

"It's possible the killer thinks she knows something and intends to silence her."

Robert inhaled a drag from the cigar. "Then shouldn't you be out looking for him?"

"We have people investigating it as we speak," Fox said.

"Good, the SOB needs to be behind bars."

Black cleared his throat. "Melissa Fagan claims she has information indicating she was Candace's daughter, but it's our understanding that you disagree."

Robert leveled a suspicious look at Black. "I see, and you think that I'd kill this woman because of her misguided ramblings."

"She has admitted that she received a threatening phone call warning her to leave town, and that you were not very cordial."

He stood. "I believe this conversation is over, gentlemen. The next time you want to ask me questions, contact me first so I can have my lawyer present."

Black and Fox both nodded. Robert waited until they had cleared the room and were outside before he called Moor. "Edward, the cops were just here. They think I tried to kill Melissa Fagan to keep her from poking into the past."

He snuffed out the cigar. "Now, if they question you next, remember—you're my alibi."

Chapter Thirteen

Melissa stewed all night over the way she'd handled Eric. She hadn't wanted to hurt him, she'd only meant to protect him. Yet the anguish she'd seen in his eyes at her comment haunted her. He hadn't deserved to be treated so poorly, not when he'd risked his life or more injuries to save her from that awful burial spot where the madman had left her.

She desperately wanted to talk to him, to apologize and declare her love, and see if he might reciprocate the feeling. Yet to keep him safe, she needed to relinquish her search for her parents.

Did it really matter who they were? She'd begun to wonder....

After all, Eric was here now. Eric hadn't abandoned her. He had pushed his own battered body beyond its limits to save her life.

Confused and aching from wanting him, she braced herself for their morning session. But when she arrived, he was already working with Helen. She paused and savored the sight, then walked over to the weight set.

"Thanks, Helen, I can take it from here."

"There's no need," Eric said in a flat voice. "Helen and I are working fine together."

Helen gave her a perplexed look. "Mr. Stinson wanted to come in early today. He didn't seem pleased with me yesterday, so maybe it's best you take him…"

She let the sentence trail off. Melissa glanced at Eric, but he kept his back to her and continued the weight lifting. Feeling bereft, as if she'd lost something more valuable than she'd first realized, she tackled her patient.

"Hi, Mr. Stinson, I'm sorry I was out yesterday."

He scowled. "Helen said someone assaulted you? Did they find the guy?"

"No, not yet." She assisted while he tried to stand, using the prosthetic leg. "But I'm sure they will."

"I hope so, Melissa. I'd hate to see anything happen to you." His gaze seemed to be probing. "I bet your folks are worried sick."

"My parents have been gone a long time." Melissa patted his arm, encouraging him to stand. She glanced back at Eric, aching all over for him, once again considering her options.

Maybe she should renounce her search. After all, if her father had murdered her mother, and would rather kill her than reveal her existence, did she really want to meet him?

ERIC POURED ALL his anger and energy into his therapy session, determined to reach his optimum physical level so he could complete this job and get the hell out of Savannah.

Whether Melissa wanted him or not, he had to protect her and arrest the man who'd tried to kill her.

But he didn't want her pity.

Her reply reverberated in his head, "That's all I have to give."

Sheer pain radiated through him, along with humiliation. Why had he believed she might want a man like him?

Because for a few minutes, she'd certainly responded as if she had....

He dismissed the mesmerizing hold she had on his body and mind, showered and returned to his cabin, then phoned Black to see if they had any leads on Hughes or Melissa's attacker.

"Nothing so far," Black said, "but we did receive fingerprint results on the CEO and that scientist, Hopkins. Apparently they're who they claim to be."

"Then neither one of the men are Hughes?"

"It appears that way, unless someone planted fake prints and covered themselves in the database."

"Is that possible?"

"Anything's possible with today's technology, but duplicity to that extent would require an insider's assistance."

Damn.

"I'd say we keep looking. Is there anyone else at CIRP who fits Hughes's profile?"

"I'll check again," Eric said. "Maybe I missed someone." He rubbed his forehead. "How about the fifth man in the photo? Did you ever find him?"

"Records say he's dead. He was killed in combat."

Eric sighed. They were no closer to finding the answers than they were when he'd first come there.

And now, he had to worry about Melissa....

"DAMN IT, I THOUGHT you killed the Fagan woman."

"I tried." He muttered a string of obscenities. "But that Collier man came to the rescue again. Who the hell is he?"

"He's working with the damn cops," the man barked. "His name is not Collier, but Caldwell."

"Caldwell?"

"Yes, the brother of the man who helped that pediatric nurse disappear with Project Simon."

"Hell, he was supposed to be dead, too."

"Someone screwed up. He almost died in that explosion, but now he's here for physical therapy working undercover. And if we don't do something, he might expose us all."

A cold chill skated up his spine. They couldn't let that happen. Not now, not when they'd just gotten more money for their research. Not when they had their own inside man at the FBI helping to ease the path for their success.

"I'll take care of both of them."

"Yeah?" A bark of disbelief followed. "Then do it right this time or I'm replacing you."

He shuddered. He knew what that meant.

Fail and die.

He wasn't ready for the end just yet, but Caldwell and Melissa Fagan had better be.

AFTER HIS SESSION, Eric reviewed the employee list at CIRP once again. Another name caught his attention—

Wallace Thacker, a chemist who'd recently transferred from the research center in Oakland, Tennessee—the facility that Cole Turner had supposedly transferred from.

Of course, Cole had been Clayton Fox, and the identity a bogus one that had been invented to give Clay a past to fit his new name and face.

Frank Chadburn, the director of that center, had also disappeared after the memory transplant experiment had been revealed.

Where was he now?

And what kind of story could Eric use to meet the chemist?

If you confided in Melissa, she might be able to help you gain access to confidential files.

No. He would not use her, especially after the way she'd dismissed him the day before.

Frustrated, he phoned Devlin to discuss a plan of action, but the agent didn't answer, so Eric left a message, grabbed his cell phone and cane and decided to take a walk. He'd make sure the guard was still posted at Melissa's.

Needing fresh air, he took the path along the beach, remembering the last time he'd walked along the shore with Melissa. The wind whistled behind him, the salty spray wetting his face with a fine mist. He felt the sting bite his cheek, then realized the sting hadn't originated from the wind, but a bullet had just grazed his face. His instincts kicking in, he pivoted to search for the shooter. In the distance on a cliff at the heart of Serpent's Cove, he spotted a man in dark clothing. The shooter fired again, this bullet zinging an inch from Eric's chest.

Eric began to run, dodging the gunfire, stumbling across the sand with his weakened legs....

MELISSA WAS WALKING back to her cottage when she spotted Eric scrambling up the embankment from the beach. What was going on? Why wouldn't he take the level path? And where was his wheelchair?

She launched into a run, forgetting about the guard. "Eric!"

The young rookie, Dothan, grabbed her arm to stop her. "Ma'am, wait."

"It's my patient, I have to see what's wrong."

Dothan nodded. "Then I'll go with you."

He followed her to the edge. Eric was struggling up the hill, his feet slipping in the sand and overgrown sea oats.

When he noticed Melissa, his eyes widened in alarm. "Melissa, get out of here!"

"Why?" She reached for his hand to help him, but he shrugged away her offer. He was only two feet from her, yet he refused to let her help him.

"I said, get out of here. There's a shooter on the cliff behind me!"

Melissa gasped and spotted a dark dot disappearing into the distance.

She turned to the guard. "Call someone to catch that man!"

Dothan phoned in, while Eric crested the hill. Melissa immediately clutched his arm. "Are you all right?'' Blood dotted his cheek. She raised a hand to wipe it away and check his wound.

"It's only a graze. Come on, let's go inside.'' Eric ushered her toward her cottage, leaning on his cane.

She slid her arm beneath his waist to give him added support, but he backed away. "I can do it,'' he growled.

"Just shut up and let's go,'' she said, refusing to let him push her away.

They hurried down the path, the guard behind them, his gun drawn as he canvassed the area for another attacker. Melissa unlocked the door, her heart pounding as they fell inside. Eric's breathing was erratic, and he favored his good leg, but at least he was alive.

She flung herself at him, checking his face and chest for injuries. "My God, Eric, he almost shot you.''

"I'm fine.''

Tears burned her eyes as she threw her arms around him. "But you could have died.''

He trapped her hands, clutching them between his own. "He didn't shoot me, Melissa. It's all right.''

Hysteria bubbled inside her. "But I thought if we weren't together, you'd be safe. Don't you see, I thought…'' She released his hands, paced across the small living area, running her fingers through her hair, her panic wild. "I wanted to protect you, but he's after you anyway. Who's doing this?''

When she paused, Eric was watching her with an intense darkness in his eyes. "Is that the reason you pushed me away? To protect me?''

Melissa realized she'd revealed herself, but the guard knocked, and Eric let him in.

"Did they catch him?" Eric asked.

Dothan shook his head. "Sorry, he escaped."

Eric nodded. "Thanks." His gaze shot back to Melissa, then to the rookie. "I'm going to stay awhile, why don't you take a break. Go for dinner."

Dothan gestured toward Melissa. "Is that all right with you, ma'am?"

"Yes, yes, of course."

Dothan excused himself, and Melissa wrapped her arms around her waist. Did she dare admit the truth to Eric and see where things led them?

ERIC HAD BOTTLED any hope that Melissa might have feelings for him, but when she'd hugged him moments ago, she hadn't acted like a woman who pitied him.

But he didn't want her guilt, either.

Eric had to know, then he'd move on. "Did you send me away the other night to protect me, or because you don't want me?"

Her gaze met his, emotions softening her eyes. He had his answer.

"I don't want your guilt, or pity," he said to clarify. "And I won't take advantage of you because you're frightened."

"I am scared," Melissa said in a low voice. "I'm scared of losing you, Eric."

His breath hitched in his throat. He'd never imagined wanting a woman the way he craved Melissa. And he'd certainly never allowed himself to believe she'd love him back, especially with his scarred body.

Then she was in his arms, hugging and holding him, and kissing him with all the fervor of a woman who had truly wanted a man for a long time. Eric cupped her face in his hands and kissed her tenderly. The flame of hunger was lit, the heat intensifying with each nibble and caress. She met his tongue thrust for thrust, seeking, yearning, silently telling him she liked his touch.

He was glad to oblige.

His soul had been dark and empty for so long that he welcomed the light. She offered it in the sweet moan that escaped her mouth as he threaded his fingers through the silky tresses of her hair. Their lips tangled and met, while her hands clutched at his arms, then skated over his back. His body hardened, the tantalizing feel of her breasts against his chest creating a slow torture inside him that ignited his arousal to a painful peak.

She surprised him by pulling back slightly and extending her hand. His breath rasped out, and he stared at her hand for a moment, then lifted her chin to look into her eyes. "Are you sure?"

A sultry smile played on her lips. "Oh, yeah, I'm sure. I want you, Eric, in my arms, in my bed, beside me."

A balloon of joy exploded in his chest, and he nodded, then followed her to the bedroom. A lamp lit the room, bathing it in a soft glow, but he flicked it off, letting the moonlight spilling through the window paint the room in a more romantic glow.

She stroked her fingers along his jaw in an erotic game that stirred his senses even more, and he kissed her again, then slowly lowered his hands to cup her breasts. They were full and heavy, hot beneath his hands as he massaged the weight. A throaty groan escaped him as he imagined baring them for his sight.

A shy look passed in her eyes that teased him even more.

"You're beautiful, Melissa. I...I wanted you the first time I saw you."

"I wanted you, too," she admitted. "But I thought it would be wrong."

"Sometimes breaking the rules is right." Grateful for the condom he kept in his wallet, he gently lifted her shirt over her head, his heart thumping as her breasts spilled over the lacy edge of a pale pink bra. Would her nipples be that pale or would they be darker, rose-tipped like the lipstick she wore?

He was dying to know, aching to feel her bare skin against his, to plunge inside her and claim her as his.

"I want to kiss you all over." He lowered his head and tasted the swell of her breasts, then lower to suck her nipples through the bra. She writhed against him, clinging to his arms to keep her balance, and he tugged the fabric down, teasing her body with his tongue and teeth. Hunger flared hotter inside him, his sex swelling and jutting toward her.

She sighed and dug her fingernails in his arms while he stripped her bra, then slipped her loose skirt to the floor. Pale pink bikini panties arched high on her slender thighs taunted him, the wisp of dark hair beneath almost sending him over the edge.

Then she pushed at his shirt, unbuttoning the first, then second button, and he stilled for the first time since he'd entered, his first signs of doubt creeping into his mind.

Melissa realized Eric's moment of hesitation but refused to allow him to hold back because of his scars. "I don't see them when I look at you," she whispered in his ear. "I see a handsome, strong man." She traced her tongue along his ear. "A man that I love."

Eric's hands cupped her face. "I...Melissa..."

"Shh, you don't have to say it back," Melissa whispered. "But I had to tell you."

He looked moved by her words as he claimed her mouth again, this kiss long and slow, tender and passionate all at the same time. Inflamed by his strength, she savored the feel of his arms around her and tugged off his shirt, running her hands over his bare back.

"You feel so wonderful, Eric."

He dropped a kiss into her hair. "Melissa, do you have any idea how much I want to make love to you?"

She smiled and kissed him. "I feel the same way."

He chuckled, and gently eased her down on the bed. But she raised herself on her knees and began to kiss his chest, tracing each scar gently with her finger, then her lips. "Tell me if I hurt you."

He cradled her head in his hands, closing his eyes and letting her heavenly touch erase the pain. "You can't." He rasped out a breath when she licked his nipple. "You won't hurt me."

Melissa prayed Eric was right. But she couldn't think of the danger right now, only that Eric might have died earlier, and she might never have had the chance to lie in his arms. She might never have made love to him.

And she desperately wanted that tonight. Wanted him to be her first.

And her last.

But she wouldn't ask for promises....

"Enough." His husky voice triggered a flood of yearning in her belly.

With a wicked gleam in his eyes, he pushed her back on the bed and kissed her again, this time hungrily, as if there would be no tomorrow. Another kiss and his hand unclasped her bra. He lowered his head and stared at her bare breasts with an almost reverent expression in his eyes. She shivered, her nipples aching pinpoints begging for his mouth.

Finally, he traced his tongue over each turgid peak and sucked them into his mouth, his greedy gulps of pleasure igniting tingling sensations through her body.

Eric fed her desires with his heady, throaty moans.

She ached to claw his back but remembered his tender skin, and restrained her urges, instead pouring them into the sounds she emitted and a desperate cry for release as sensations built within her. His fingers danced down her belly, followed by his tongue, and when he dipped them inside her panties, skimming them along her heat, she thought she might die.

Ripple after ripple of pleasure soared through her as he gently stroked her inner thighs, then slid down her body and placed his tongue to the sensitive skin between her legs. His breath caressed her heat while his tongue tortured her with teasing delicious strokes. And when he tasted her, she bucked upward, crying out his name in euphoric release.

EMOTIONS WELLED inside Eric like a tidal wave as Melissa's body convulsed in his arms. She tasted like fire and sweetness, her declaration of love completely stunning him.

No one had ever loved him before except his brother.

Aching for fulfillment, he wrestled the condom from his wallet, pulled it over his length, rose above her and braced his arms by her sides, then teased her legs farther apart with his good leg and slid his erection against her heat. She whimpered and lifted her hips, begging him to enter her, and he thrust inside with a moan.

Her tightness surprised him.

Her virginity shocked him.

"Melissa..." He stilled, but she pressed her hands to his cheeks and dragged his mouth toward hers.

"Please, Eric, I have to have you."

Heaven sent down a shooting star that obliterated any misgivings. He knew he should mouth loving words back, but he was so humbled by her offering, he could only kiss her, thrusting his tongue deep into her mouth as he thrust his sex into her welcoming heat. He hesitated, giving her time to adjust to his size, but she moaned and moved below him, pulling him deeper and deeper inside her until he'd filled her to the core.

Unable to control his fierce longing for another moment, he began to pump inside her, in and out, teasing her to the edge of another orgasm and himself to insanity.

"I do love you, Eric," she whispered as release swept her into a trembling mass.

He fell into the vortex with her, soaring, soaring, soaring....

ERIC CRADLED MELISSA in his arms, the titillating sensations still rippling through him. He'd never experienced such intensity with a woman, such closeness. He wanted to wrap her in his arms and keep the two of them buried in this warm cocoon of bliss forever.

But they had to talk. He should say something, confess his feelings, only they were so new and foreign to him, his emotions so raw that his voice refused to cooperate. He had been so angry and confused and lost when his mother died, and after the explosion. He'd thought he was meant to protect others, to get revenge. Never had he considered that he might have a normal life, a woman to love him....

He wanted that normal life. He wanted to be with Melissa forever.

She gently traced a finger over his chest and his heart swelled with such longing that he cleared his throat to tell her, but a knock sounded at the door. Damn it, he didn't want to answer.

But what if the police had found the shooter? What if they had the break in the case and he could put it to rest, lock Hughes away and start looking toward a future?

Melissa sighed as the knocking grew louder. "I should get it, I guess."

He shook his head. "No, stay here. I'll go."

She bit down on her lip, but relented. He stood, dragged on his jeans and shirt, grabbed his cane, then headed to the living area, closing the bedroom door to give her privacy. He hurriedly buttoned his shirt, not ready to share his newfound relationship with the guard.

But Special Agent Devlin stood on the other side, looking harried and in a rush. "We have to talk."

Eric jammed his hands in his pockets. "What are you doing here?"

"Black filled me in on the shooting. Listen, Eric, we need to move on this investigation."

"Why?"

"Word is that Hughes has not only resurfaced but that he has scientists working on brainwashing techniques."

"You knew that all along."

"Yes, but we think he's using unsuspecting patients as guinea pigs. And we're almost certain Hughes is Melissa Fagan's father."

Eric's stomach knotted. "How can you be sure?"

Devlin's moment of hesitation sparked Eric's suspicion. "You knew before. That's why you sent me here, arranged to have me work with Melissa." Anger tightened his throat. "You set me up, didn't you?"

Guilt flashed in Devlin's eyes for a millisecond before he masked it.

"We had no way of being sure you'd actually meet her, but I did some checking when you mentioned you had, and we finally hacked into the old files." Devlin's voice was level. "Believe it or not, Hughes was actually listed on the birth certificate of the baby Candace Latone delivered."

Eric let that fact sink in. What would Melissa think? How would she react if she learned her father was a monster? He had to protect her from the truth. "So, Robert Latone lied about his daughter having a child?"

"He not only lied, he personally dropped the baby at the church."

The door squeaked open, and Melissa stepped into the entryway. Eric's pulse clamored at the yellowish tint to her pallor. Apparently, she'd been listening to their conversation.

Just how much had she heard?

Chapter Fourteen

A cold numbness enveloped Melissa as she stared at the man who had taken her in his arms and joined his body with hers, the man she had proclaimed that she loved.

He obviously wasn't the man she believed him to be. And his heart had not been in the joining.

Who was he?

"What's going on?" she asked in a surprisingly calm voice. Her body was trembling from the inside out, still adjusting from lying sated in Eric's arms to the shock of betrayal.

His dark eyes flickered downward in avoidance. Regret. Guilt.

The suited man with dark blond hair started to speak, but Eric threw up a hand. "Let me explain."

Melissa folded her arms across her waist, wishing she'd had the good sense to dress instead of slipping on her robe. She felt raw, exposed. Vulnerable. And she hated it.

"This is Special Agent Luke Devlin, Melissa, he's with the FBI."

She swallowed hard. "And you are?"

His gaze met hers. "Eric Caldwell."

A knot of pain clogged her throat. "So you lied about your name?"

He gave a clipped nod. "But there are reasons."

She cut a sharp gaze toward the federal agent, then back at Eric, a sickening thought emerging. "You're an FBI agent?"

Eric shook his head. "Not exactly." He scrubbed his hand through his hair, eliciting memories of when he'd run his hands through her own. Nausea climbed to her throat. "I…I have been working with them. So have Detectives Black and Fox."

"I don't understand. To find Candace's murderer?" Had Eric suspected her as the killer? Had he cozied up to her to find out?

"Yes, and to investigate CIRP."

"We have reason to believe Arnold Hughes has re-surfaced," Agent Devlin interjected.

Melissa pieced together the remnants of the conversation she'd overheard, the truth dawning in all its ugly details. "And you think he's my father?" She pierced Eric with a cold look. "That's the reason you warmed up to me, to find him?"

Eric's silence said it all. The closeness she'd felt earlier disintegrated, the pain of his lie engulfing her.

"Why do you want him so badly?" she asked, her voice a mere whisper.

"You've heard about the things he did," Devlin answered. "He's responsible for the loss of several people's lives, unethical experiments, using prisoners as human guinea pigs. He ordered memory transplant experiments to be performed on Detective Fox. Who knows what other twisted games he has in the works.''

''And he might have killed Candace Latone,'' Eric added in a gruff voice.

She met Eric's haunted gaze, her breath locked in her chest as she read between the lines. There was something he wasn't telling her, something more personal. His hand brushed his hair back, revealing the scar on his forehead, and she realized the truth. ''Your accident?''

''It wasn't an accident.'' He closed his eyes, the bleakness she'd seen before returning when he opened them. ''I was trying to help one of his nurses escape from Nighthawk Island. She was rescuing a baby his scientists had involved in an experiment.''

''A baby? Oh my God.'' Her legs collapsed. Eric reached for her, but she pushed his hands away and staggered to the couch. Her head spinning, she dropped it forward into her hands and sucked in air, ordering herself not to pass out.

Hughes, a madman with no scruples, was her father? He had killed countless people, played with their lives, tried to kill Eric. And he might have murdered Candace?

Why? Because he thought Candace might reveal that Hughes was Melissa's father?

Had her own father tried to kill her?

A chill engulfed her. Eric had known the truth about Hughes all along.

Worse, he had never cared for her. He'd only used her to find Hughes for his own vengeful purposes.

And being the lost desperate-for-love soul she'd

been, she'd played right into his hands like a puppet on a string.

She'd not only offered him her love, she'd given him her virginity.

ERIC DESPISED THE LOOK of anguish and betrayal in Melissa's eyes. If only he'd told her he loved her, confided the truth earlier, maybe she'd understand. He could have cushioned the blow.

He wanted to take her in his arms and make her understand, but Devlin's condemning look halted his confession.

He knew Eric had crossed the line, had slept with her.

And Eric could not let his personal feelings compromise the mission.

"We have reason to believe Robert Latone is working with Hughes," Devlin said, breaking into his confused thoughts. "And we think Hughes is overseeing brainwashing experiments on psychiatric patients without their knowledge. He's not only training them as spies and hit men for the government, but also for his own purposes."

"You think one of them was the shooter who fired at me from the cliff?"

Devlin nodded. "We also have reason to believe he might be planning to leave the country soon."

"How do you know all this?" Eric asked.

"I can't reveal my source's name, it's too dangerous, but the information is reliable."

Melissa toyed with her robe belt. "How...was my mother involved with Hughes?"

"There were experiments with infertility drugs in place at the time, as well as various birth control pills and in vitro fertilization," Devlin explained. "We believe Candace had an affair with Hughes, and that she took an experimental form of birth control pill. We also believe she experienced an adverse reaction to the drug."

"It caused her mental problems," Melissa filled in.

Devlin shrugged. "It's possible."

"Do you think it was passed to me, that the drug might have caused my seizures?"

"It might have been a side effect, yes."

Melissa rubbed her forehead, a headache pinching. "You think Hughes and Robert Latone conspired to kill me because they were afraid I'd figure out what they'd done to Candace?"

Eric stared at her, seeing the horror in her eyes. Not only had her father and grandfather abandoned her, now they'd killed her mother and tried to murder her. The depth of their evil was almost impossible to comprehend, even for a jaded man like himself who'd seen terrible things parents inflicted on their children.

"Our theory is that Hughes and Latone have been working together."

"But why would Robert Latone want to keep the drug's problems quiet if the drug affected his daughter adversely?" Melissa asked.

Eric cleared his throat. "Money. If he'd funded the experimental project, he'd want to keep it quiet."

"Even at the expense of his daughter's health?"

"We're talking millions. We think they'd already sold the pill to some foreign countries, and if word had leaked that the drug had adverse reactions, the deal would have been killed,'' Devlin continued.

"It's also possible that Hughes doesn't know you are his daughter," Eric said quietly. "Latone could have forced Candace to give you up without telling the father."

"That would be another reason Latone would want you dead. If he kept your identity from Hughes all these years, chances are Hughes would retaliate against him. Of all people, Latone knows how ruthless Hughes can be.''

Melissa knotted her hands together, her mind reeling. Her father, her grandfather, both despicable men. Poor Candace… "How do you plan to catch Hughes?"

Devlin telegraphed his silent suggestion to Eric, but Eric shook his head.

"What?" Melissa asked, confused. "Can't you drag Robert Latone in and force him to talk?"

"We've questioned him, but he lawyered up."

Melissa saw the awkward look pass between the men again and put two and two together. She wanted this to end so she could return to Atlanta. And Hughes and Latone should pay for what they had done to her mother. "I could help trap Hughes."

Eric stalked toward her, arms crossed. "Absolutely not."

Melissa squared her shoulders, refusing to back down. "You have nothing to say about it."

"It's too dangerous, Melissa. We'll find another way."

"You lied to me, Eric, why should I listen to you now?"

His mask slipped slightly, raw emotion darkening his eyes. "Because I refuse to let you act as bait for a madman." He curled his fingers around her wrist, then lowered his voice. "I care about you, Melissa. I don't want you in danger."

"It's too late for that." She hesitated, hating the crack in her voice. "Besides, if you cared so much, you would have been honest."

"Damn it, Melissa, you can't do this."

"I don't need your permission." She turned to the federal agent, her resolve in place. If these men thought she'd crumble, they were wrong. She'd been on her own, survived foster care and her teenage years alone. She would survive this, too.

"Agent Devlin, tell me what to do."

A STEELY RAGE BLAZED through Eric as Devlin detailed the plan. Melissa hadn't looked at him once. She'd drawn a curtain over her emotions and shut him out.

He recognized the signs because he'd used the same coping skill countless times in his own life.

The fact that he had hurt her badly enough to send her back into that isolated darkness made him feel lower than he'd ever felt.

"I'll leak the story to the press," Devlin explained. "Say the police questioned you regarding Candace Latone's murder, and you admitted that you were searching for your parents, Candace Latone and Arnold Hughes. With all the publicity about CIRP in the past, the story should make front page.''

''And how will we arrange for him to meet me?''

''Oh, he'll come looking,'' Devlin said. ''And we'll be ready.''

''You never make a mistake, do you?'' Eric glared at the agent, remembering other missions gone awry, the reason he'd taken the law into his own hands a few times. The reason he'd been protecting that witness in the Bronsky case.

He wanted to protect Melissa now.

Because he'd fallen in love.

Unfortunately, she was barreling forward, putting her own life on the line because he'd hurt her.

God, what a mess.

''We'll have plenty of backup,'' Devlin said. ''In fact, I'll guard you personally, Miss Fagan.''

Melissa exhaled. ''Then let's do it.''

Devlin nodded.

''I'll be with her at all times,'' Eric said.

''No.'' Melissa's condemning look cut him to the quick. ''One agent will be enough.''

''I'm not leaving you alone,'' Eric said. He directed his next comment to Devlin. ''And if you don't agree with that, she's out of this completely.''

Devlin frowned. ''Are you sure you're up to it, Caldwell?''

Anger flared inside Eric. Another agent would be stronger, more agile. ''Yes,'' he said anyway. ''I started this investigation and I'm seeing it through.''

''The story should run tomorrow,'' Devlin said.

Melissa nodded.

Devlin yanked Eric's arm, pulling him outside. "You need to let us handle things from here on out."

Eric pried the agent's fingers from his arm. "You think I can't take care of myself if it gets rough?"

"I think you're too damn involved with the woman." Devlin scraped his hair back from his forehead. "It's obvious you slept with her."

Eric gritted his teeth, ready to deny it.

"You're not objective, man, and she sure as hell isn't objective where you're concerned." He lowered his voice, his tone lethal. "Her safety is my priority."

"It had better be." For a brief second, Eric vacillated, though, wondered if Devlin was right about his ability to protect Melissa. What if someone attacked her, and he failed to fight them off? What if he let her down and he lost her forever?

His mother's bloody body flashed into his mind.

No, Melissa was nothing like his mother. She was a fighter, she was tough and strong, and he would give his life to protect her.

He didn't trust anyone else to keep her safe.

ROBERT LATONE ACCEPTED coffee from his maid, claimed his usual chair on the veranda and unfolded the morning paper. His gaze landed on the headlines, and his chest spasmed. Dear God in heaven, he couldn't believe the Fagan woman had talked to the press. And to publicly claim Candace her mother and Hughes her father—was she on a suicide mission?

Fury rattling his movements, he jerked up and stalked inside. Moor marched through the front door, his face livid, before Robert could even call him.

"Have you seen the paper?" Moor asked.

"Hell, yes." Robert slapped it on the cherry table-top. "I thought you were handling the Fagan woman."

"I tried." Moor wiped sweat from his graying eye-brow.

"What are we going to do now?" Robert shrieked. "If Hughes reads this, he'll be all over my ass."

Moor's fingers trembled as he spread his palms on top of the article. "I'll think of something, Robert. Don't worry. No one will ever find out the truth."

"Talk to Hopkins."

Moor's pallor had turned a chalky gray. "I'm on it."

"Right away," Latone hissed. "And don't screw up this time. We can't let this go any further."

Moor unpocketed his cell phone and began to punch in numbers. "Hopkins, meet me at the marina in half an hour. I have a job for you."

Latone jabbed in numbers on his own phone. He had to make arrangements to leave the country. It was bad enough the police suspected him of killing his own daughter. When Hughes read the article, he would think Robert had betrayed him.

And he didn't intend to take the repercussions of Hughes's wrath.

"MELISSA FAGAN, PLEASE."

Melissa's fingers tightened around the handset. Eric lifted his head from where he'd been reading notes on Hughes from Devlin's ongoing file. "This is she."

"Do you really want to meet your father?"

She swallowed hard, motioning at Eric to trace the call.

"Then come to the marina. Tonight. Midnight." His heavy breathing wheezed over the line. "And come alone, Melissa."

"Who—" Melissa's voice broke at the sound of the dial tone.

Devlin shook his head. "Not enough time to get a trace."

Eric muttered a curse. Melissa ignored him. He didn't like the setup, had tried to persuade her to back out, but Melissa refused to be a quitter.

Besides, she wanted this quest for her parents to be over. Every second in proximity with Eric made his deception even more painful.

"What did the caller want?" Eric asked.

"He said if I wanted to meet my father to come to the marina tonight at midnight."

Devlin nodded. "This could be the break we've been waiting for."

And the day she'd anticipated forever—meeting her father.

Only, instead of walking into his loving arms, she might be walking into a trap.

And instead of finding a loving father, she would be looking at the face of the man who'd killed her mother, and wanted her buried in the ground beside Candace.

TREPIDATION FILLED ERIC as they drove to the marina. He had worked out all morning, strengthening his arms and legs, and channeling his energy so he would be able to help tonight. He couldn't fail Melissa, not any more than he already had.

When they caught Hughes, he'd rectify his past mistakes with Melissa. He had no idea how, but he'd find some way to convince her that he loved her.

She looked frail and strong at the same time as she braced herself for the confrontation he knew would follow. If the meeting turned out to be a trap, they were prepared. Devlin had stationed two other agents around the marina, patrolling the area in advance, one disguised as a fisherman, another a local tourist.

A spring thunderstorm loomed on the horizon, thunderclouds obliterating the stars and adding an even more ominous feel to the gloomy atmosphere. The sound of docked boats rocking in the increasingly turbulent water mingled with the occasional whine of a motor. Eric hung back, hidden in the shadows of a cruiser, his senses charged.

Melissa's shoes clicked on the boardwalk as she paced to the end of the dock and stared out at the water. A ten-foot cruiser coasted by. Odd for it to be out this time of night.

It had to be the caller.

Eric stepped forward to warn Melissa, but the boat coasted to a stop, and Devlin waved him to hold off. Eric was too far away, Devlin even farther. Where were the two other agents?

Suddenly gunfire rang out, and all hell broke loose behind him. He pivoted and saw the first agent go down in a bloody heap. The fisherman/agent was nowhere to be seen. Devlin fired his gun, warding off the shooter, while Eric hobbled down the dock as fast as his cane would allow him.

A man grabbed Melissa, but she swung her fists at him. Another appeared out of nowhere and assaulted Eric, bringing him down with a whack on the back of the head. More gunfire pinged behind him. He clawed at the wooden slats to right himself, but a karate punch to his lower back and a blow to his ribs knocked the air from his lungs. Then something hard connected with his head. The blunt end of a gun.

Melissa screamed, her voice fading into the darkness as Eric lost consciousness.

Chapter Fifteen

Melissa stirred, her vision blurring as she struggled to discern what had happened on the dock. A rocking motion spiked nausea, the sound of a motor humming from above alerting her to the fact that she was on a boat. She turned her head, squinting through the darkness. She was in a small berth on the bottom level. Her arms and legs were bound, but her captors hadn't gagged her, which either meant that they hadn't expected her to regain consciousness or they were so far away from shore no one would hear if she screamed.

She fought hopelessness. The room faded, then cleared again, and she spotted Eric on the floor in the corner. He lay sideways, blood trickling from his head, his face ghostly white.

Please don't let him be dead.

She shifted and scooted across the floor, each movement causing her stomach to capitulate. "Eric." She finally reached him, and nudged him with her foot. "Eric, wake up."

He stirred slightly, and she nudged him again. "Eric, wake up, tell me you're all right."

A moan rumbled from his chest, and he slowly

opened his eyes. He looked disoriented as he lifted his head. Blood trickled from his forehead down his jaw.

"Are you okay?" Melissa whispered.

He nodded. "What about you?"

"Yes, but we have to get out of here."

He glanced around the cabin. "Do you know where they're taking us?"

"No."

"Did you see Hughes?"

"No, some guy grabbed me and knocked me out, but he was too young to be Hughes."

"Hired help," Eric growled. "I'm sorry, Melissa. I never should have let you go through with this."

"I made my own choice, Eric."

"But I should have protected you." He dropped his head forward, his voice anguished. "My mother...I couldn't protect her, and now you."

Melissa had no idea what he meant about his mother, but explanations had to wait. They needed to escape. "Do you think you can untie me?"

He nodded. "Roll over, put your back to me."

She did as he said, and he flipped himself over, so his own bound hands could reach hers. For the next several minutes, they lay in tense silence as Eric struggled to unravel the thick knots.

"Damn it, I need a knife." He glanced around the cabin, but barring a small foldout sofa-type bed, it appeared empty. Shifting again, he tried the knots once more.

"Tell me what you meant about your mother," Melissa whispered in an attempt to fill the dreadful silence.

"My father, he abused her," Eric said in a voice that echoed with old pain. "She finally gave up one day and killed herself."

"She left you and your brother alone to face him?"

Eric stilled for a moment. "Yeah. I always blamed myself, though. I've been helping women escape situations like that for years through an underground service. That's the reason my brother's wife, Alanna, came to me when she and baby Simon were in trouble."

So the job on his patient file was bogus. "Do you work for an agency?"

"No, I'm on my own."

She closed her eyes, letting the truth wash over her. He wasn't a cop or a federal agent, but a really good guy. No wonder she had connected with him. And fallen in love.

Still, he'd used her and lied to her. And he hadn't once mentioned loving her in return.

Even if he had feelings for her, would he blame her for what her father had done to him?

ERIC HAD ALMOST GOTTEN the first knot untangled, when the boat slowed and the motor died. They had docked. He hoped Devlin or one of the other agents had survived and followed them. It might be their only chance to get out of this alive.

The door swung open, and a beefy man sporting tattoos up and down his arms entered, a Glock in his hand—the man he'd seen leaving Hopkins's office.

Melissa tensed and curled closer to him, but the man jerked Eric upright. His bad leg buckled, and he fought through the pain, but the man kicked the back of Eric's kneecap, and he nearly crumpled.

"Stop it!" Melissa cried.

"It's time," the man mumbled.

Eric offered Melissa a silent look, telling her he would be all right, but the man pressed the gun to his head, then dragged him out the door.

Melissa's terrified cries rang through the thin doorway as the man hauled him up the steps. Seconds later, the sound of a hawk soaring above made him jerk his head up, and he scanned the area. He was on Nighthawk Island.

He had no idea who had kidnapped them, but he doubted he would leave the island alive.

Why were they separating him and Melissa? Why not kill them together?

His captor shoved him into a dark sedan and slammed the door. Five minutes later, the car stopped, and he was dragged into a lab. The building was small, with several other labs along the hall, all sterile and functional with Restricted warning signs. One sign noted possible biohazard materials, another germ warfare. The lab was filled with petri dishes and appeared to be a hot room for growing germs.

The man shoved him onto a gurney, then a doctor garbed in sterile attire, mask and gloves included, moved above him, a hypodermic in hand. Hopkins?

"Now we'll find out how strong your willpower is, Mr. Caldwell. See if you can resist our techniques."

Eric recognized Hopkins's voice.

"What are you planning to do to me?" Eric asked.

"Brainwash you to do our dirty work." Hopkins laughed. "Then our hands will be clean."

Eric had to escape. He fought against the ropes, then bucked upward, trying to knock the needle from the doctor's hand, but the beefy man who'd dragged him in pounced on his throbbing leg. Another man restrained his arms, and the doctor fed him the shot.

MELISSA CURLED INTO A BALL, hopelessness engulfing her. Eric was gone. They'd taken him at gunpoint hours ago.

He was probably dead.

The anguish that consumed her was overwhelming.

You have to fight back. You've been on your own before, you can do it again.

Yet the thought of going on, knowing Eric had been murdered, nearly paralyzed her.

The boat rocked and swayed where they'd docked. Why hadn't they come to kill her yet? Was Hughes behind the kidnapping, or had someone intervened to keep her from knowing his identity? The man who'd dragged Eric from the cabin was obviously a hired gun. Had he murdered her mother?

The door swung open and fear knifed through her.

She was shocked to see Eric at the door.

Relief made her giddy, but evaporated when she spoke his name and he didn't respond. His eyes were glazed, his pupils dilated, his posture stiff as if he hadn't heard her. She glanced behind him, searching for the gun man, but saw no one.

"Eric, hurry, untie me."

He didn't acknowledge her plea. Instead, he continued to stare into empty space, like a robot.

"Hurry, before they come back."

He stalked toward her. Then he jerked her up by her bound arms and began to drag her up the steps. Fear replaced her earlier relief.

"Eric, what are you doing? Talk to me!" Panic made her words shrill. "Stop it, Eric, you're hurting me. Tell me what's going on."

He gripped her arm tighter, then dragged her off the boat. Her toes scattered broken shells in the path. Darkness shrouded the island, and a screeching sound echoed in the distance as if a wild animal had cornered its prey.

Melissa understood the feeling.

She cringed at the vacant look in Eric's eyes. He'd obviously been drugged, but what else had they done to him?

Had the scientists destroyed Eric's memory as they had done to that cop?

"Walk ahead." His command sounded harsh, his voice deeper than Eric's as he pushed her forward. She stumbled, her bound legs making it impossible to walk.

"Untie me, Eric, and we can run."

He hauled her forward, then shoved her through the underbrush until they reached a clearing on the cliff.

"Eric, you're scaring me. What's going on? What did they do to you?"

He stared straight ahead, his mouth a flat line. Finally he spoke, his tone lethal. "You have to die."

Fear chilled Melissa's spine. The scientists had hypnotized him. She had to bring him back, to save him. Both of them.

He pulled out a gun, and she froze. She was going to die.

And whoever had drugged Eric had somehow convinced him to do the killing.

But how? Why?

To frame him...

"Eric, you don't want to hurt me." She struggled to maintain a calm voice, afraid a panicked cry might trigger whatever hypnotic suggestion they'd given him. It had to be a hypnotic suggestion, that was the only explanation that made sense.

But she didn't think a person could be hypnotized against his will.

He aimed the gun at her. "It will be over soon."

Melissa shivered. He spoke in a monotone, like someone programmed to kill her. Was that part of the research on Nighthawk Island? Were the scientists hypnotizing, brainwashing men to be trained assassins, to kill on demand?

She had to jar him from this trance. "Eric, you don't want to do this," she said softly. "You know you don't. You're a good man, a protector. Remember, you wanted to save your mother from pain, but you couldn't." She inhaled. "You helped all those other women escape their abusive husbands and boyfriends. You could never hurt a woman."

His jaw tightened, his eyes flickering, as if her words had registered on some distant plane.

"You have a brother, Cain, you told me about him and his wife. And they have a son, Simon, isn't that his name?'' She was grasping now, determined to reach him. ''You came to CIRP to find Arnold Hughes and make him pay for hurting other people because you're not evil like them. You can't hurt anyone, you protect and save others. You helped me.''

His hand shook slightly, the gun wobbling.

''Remember me, I'm Melissa. We worked together to teach you to walk again. And now you don't need the wheelchair anymore. We made love the other night, Eric. I lay in your arms and you held me and we kissed....''

He blinked, his eyes flittering sideways, his body wavering.

''Remember how sweet it was, Eric. I whispered that I love you, then we made slow beautiful love together in my cottage. It was tender and passionate, and we wanted the night to last forever.''

The gun lowered slightly and hope dawned, featherlight but alive.

''I kissed your scars, made them disappear, because when I'm with you, I don't see them, I see only a strong man who's always protected the weaker ones around him. You tried to rescue your mother, your clients and me. You didn't want me to set a trap for Hughes because you wanted to keep me safe, Eric, not hurt me.'' She inched forward, although she couldn't walk more than baby steps.

''You told me you care about me, and you wanted to keep me from being hurt again. I am safe, Eric, safe when I'm in your arms.''

His hand trembled, the mask on his face slipping. She had him, she just had to keep talking.

But a man appeared in the background, hidden in the shadows.

"Shoot her, Caldwell. You've been trained to be a killer, now carry out your orders."

Melissa's heart sank as he raised the gun and aimed.

"YOU'RE A KILLER, you've been trained to shoot." Eric heard the words. They were true.

He had killed before. Memories of a car explosion splintered through his brain. A man begging for his help, for mercy. Eric watching him die.

And then there were fights. His own father. Other men. Holding a gun on someone. His brother, the cops, hounding at the door to stop him.

"Eric, please, hear me now, it's Melissa. I love you, you don't want to hurt me."

"Do it, Caldwell. You have a job to do. Finish it." Yes, he had a job to do. The reason he'd come to this island. To get revenge. He had to complete the mission.

He angled the gun, aimed.

"Eric, think about your mother. What would she want you to do? Think about Cain, his wife. We could have that, too. A family."

The voice—Melissa? She sounded so familiar. He knew her....

No, he had lost her. He had done something bad to her, she hated him.

"Kill her. Go ahead and shoot," the man ordered.

"You're not a killer. You're a protector, a savior," Melissa whispered. "You aren't bad like them, Eric. Don't let them win."

He walked both sides of the law. And he had used his fists before on another man....

"You're good, Eric. That's the reason I fell in love with you." Melissa's whispers called to him, reaching through the murky haze to his soul. "I want us to be together."

"She's lying, Caldwell. Do it. Do it now."

"No, Eric...I love you."

Eric's hand trembled, but he aimed the gun, pressed the trigger and fired.

MELISSA DROPPED to the ground, the sound of gunfire rippling through the air, stealing her breath. For a split second, she thought she'd been shot, then realized that Eric had pivoted when he fired and hit the man behind him. She tasted dirt and tried to stand, but her chin scraped the ground with her feeble attempt. A helicopter roared above and descended into the clearing. Two men rushed through the underbrush. Eric seemed transfixed, his gaze focused on the bleeding man on the ground.

"Eric, hurry, untie me!"

He suddenly spun around, saw her and started toward her, but another gunshot rang out and his body jolted, then hit the dirt.

"No!"

"Melissa!" He barely raised his head, his voice a raspy whisper.

Two men stalked toward Melissa, jerked her up and dragged her toward a dark sedan that appeared from nowhere.

She screamed for Eric, but another man emerged from the sedan.

"Miss Fagan?"

She gulped, shocked. She recognized him from the center. "What? Who are you?"

"I'm Arnold Hughes. I need to know if you're really my daughter."

Chapter Sixteen

Pain needled Eric's side where the bullet had pierced him, but he rolled sideways and sat up. Dear God, he'd almost killed Melissa.

He pressed his hand to stem the blood and searched the space to find her.

A dark sedan had driven up, a driver stood beside the vehicle and another man—Stinson, the war vet with the artificial leg—faced Melissa. What the hell was going on?

He quickly checked behind him. Hopkins was still down.

The sound of another chopper spun above him, and the trees and dirt rustled with its landing.

"Melissa!"

Stinson grabbed her arm and shoved her into the sedan. Eric vaulted upward and stood, blood dripping down his side, but his bad leg buckled, throbbing where his attacker had kicked it earlier. Damn it. He would never make it.

Through the clearing, voices sounded, and Detectives Black and Fox jogged toward them, weapons drawn. Devlin approached, too, his wounded arm in a sling. Two other agents circled the vehicle.

"It's over," Devlin shouted to the driver. "Put your hands up and surrender."

Stinson gripped the car door and glanced at Eric, then Devlin and the surrounding cops and agents, his expression grim. "Hold your fire."

Devlin trained his weapon on Stinson, a heartbeat of silence following. But Stinson shocked everyone by raising his hands and surrendering without a fight. "You can take me in, but don't shoot. I don't want Melissa harmed."

Eric frowned and hobbled closer while Devlin handcuffed Stinson and his driver. Black radioed for a stretcher for Hopkins.

Melissa climbed from the car, and Eric met her gaze.

Guilt slammed into him as he remembered holding a gun on her. Her face looked pained, but she started toward him. "Eric?"

He held his side, his emotions torn. He wanted to drag her into his arms and make sure she was all right. But how could she forgive him for almost killing her?

"What's Stinson got to do with this?" he asked.

She bit down on her lip. "He claims he's Arnold Hughes. He wanted to know if he's my father."

MELISSA RECOGNIZED the anguish in Eric's eyes and understood he blamed himself for what had happened earlier. Her own head was spinning from the ordeal and from shock at learning the man she'd been helping with therapy was actually Arnold Hughes.

She reached out to Eric, but he drew back. Detective Black approached him. "We need to get you to the hospital."

Eric nodded. "Hopkins?"

"He'll make it. I can't wait to interrogate him and Stinson, though."

Eric frowned, his body growing weaker. Fox met Melissa and guided her to the helicopter, and a few minutes later, they were in the air.

"We need to stop his bleeding," Melissa said.

Black found some bandages and gauze from the emergency kit. "Here, will this work?"

Melissa nodded, removed the items and tore his shirt. Eric froze, riddled with pain and shame. He didn't deserve her care.

She pressed gauze to his wound, then applied pressure to stem the bleeding, and wrapped his side with bandages, her gaze meeting his. "You saved my life," she whispered.

He shook his head, hating himself. "I almost killed you."

"You were brainwashed, Eric. You didn't kill me, because you couldn't. You shot Hopkins instead."

Eric closed his eyes, wanting to believe her, but images of the fear in Melissa's eyes when he had pointed the gun at her face haunted him. He'd been violent. Evil. Out of control.

People could fight hypnosis, brainwashing, if they were strong. Hopkins never could have forced him to be a killer if he didn't already possess an inherent dark side.

The images would stay with him forever.

"I want testing done," he heard Melissa say to Detective Black. "I have to know if Mr. Stinson is Arnold Hughes, and if he's my real father."

"We'll run tests right away," Black assured her.

Eric grimaced as he realized their mistake—they had searched all of CIRP's personnel records, but it had never occurred to him or the other agents that Hughes might be at the center as a patient. And Stinson was the name of the war veteran in the picture, the missing man.

Fox cleared his throat. "We're also bringing in Robert Latone and his friend, Edward Moor, for further questioning."

"Who killed Candace?" Melissa asked.

"Don't worry, Miss Fagan," Black assured her. "Now that we have Hughes in custody, we'll get the rest of the answers."

MELISSA PACED the waiting room while Eric was in surgery. He had looked so desolate and alone when they'd wheeled him into the E.R., so distant. As if he'd already decided to end their relationship.

She pieced together her own emotions. He had lied to her and used her when he'd first come to CIRP, and she'd been hurt. But he'd had good reasons. Hughes had caused the explosion that had killed Eric's witness and nearly killed him.

But how did Dr. Hopkins play into it all? Why would he brainwash Eric to kill her?

Eric...admittedly he had frightened her. But he hadn't hurt her. Could he move past the incident on the island and possibly love her?

"Miss Fagan?"

Melissa startled and turned to see a tall dark-haired man and a woman holding a baby. "Yes?"

"I'm Cain Caldwell, Eric's brother." Cain gestured toward the woman. "This is my wife, Alanna, and our son, Simon."

Melissa smiled. "Yes, Eric told me all about you."

Cain's eyebrows rose. "Really?"

"Yes." She played with the baby's hand. "Hey, Simon, your uncle is so proud of you." One day she'd like to have a little boy of her own. Maybe one who looked like Eric.

"Yeah, Simon's pretty special." Cain grinned, the goofy proud look of a father. "How's my brother?"

"He's in surgery now. The bullet pierced his abdomen."

"How about you?" Alanna asked softly.

Melissa shrugged. "Shaken, but okay." She glanced back to Cain. "Did you know the reason Eric was here?"

"Yes, although I was against Eric working undercover," Cain admitted. "But my brother can be pretty damn stubborn."

"That stubborn nature helped him learn to walk again, it should get him through surgery, too," Melissa said. Although, it might prevent him from forgiving himself.

Alanna jiggled the baby on her hip. "You want to fill us in on what happened?"

Melissa folded her arms across her stomach and relayed the ordeal. "Eric blames himself for the brainwashing," Melissa said. She gave his brother a pleading look. "But he wouldn't hurt me," she said, staring down at her knotted hands. "He couldn't, he's too much of a protector."

Alanna curved a comforting arm around Melissa.

"Let's just hope we can convince him of that," Cain said.

The doctor appeared in the doorway. "Miss Fagan?"

"Yes." She gestured toward Cain and his wife and introduced them.

"How's my brother?" Cain asked.

"Mr. Caldwell came through surgery fine. He'll need some time to recover, but he'll be all right."

He would be physically, but what about his mental and emotional state?

When she and Cain and Alanna entered the room to see him a few minutes later, her fears were confirmed. Eric refused to look at her.

And the soul-deep anguish and loneliness she'd seen in him when they'd first met had returned.

THE NEXT TWO DAYS were torture for Eric. Not only did his side throb like the devil, but so did his leg. And he missed Melissa.

She had stopped by to visit, but he had refused to see her. How could he look into her eyes after almost killing her? She deserved a good strong, whole man, not a scarred one who possessed a dangerous side.

"You're crazy," Cain told him. "That woman loves you."

"Let it go," Eric told his brother. "I'm not interested."

"Then why the hell do you look like you lost your best friend?" Cain asked.

Alanna rocked Simon in her arms. "I may be new to the family, Eric, but you deserve some happiness for a change."

"That's right," Cain said. "You've served your penance for Mom's death."

"This has nothing to do with her." In fact, he'd realized how much stronger Melissa was than their mother. She had been weak, even selfish in giving up, in leaving her boys alone to fend for themselves.

Melissa never gave up—she was a fighter.

"Go after her," Cain said.

"Just drive me to the station," Eric said. "I want to be there when they interrogate Latone and Moor." The Feds had caught Latone and Moor trying to escape the country the night before. Hughes had given in to a DNA test and they were waiting for results. So far, Hughes had admitted to his other crimes, and that he had overseen the brainwashing experiments. The police had also found the tattooed man who'd been brainwashed and had him in custody.

Cain shook his head, a disgusted look on his face, but he and Eric headed outside, then Cain drove him.

"Shouldn't Melissa be here?" Cain asked as they seated themselves in the interrogation room.

"Let's see what we find," Eric said, determined to cushion the blow for her.

He cornered Devlin before they started. "How did Hopkins and his men know who we were and where we were meeting Hughes?"

"We have a leak in the FBI. We don't know who

yet, but someone is working both sides, us and CIRP." Devlin excused himself to meet with Latone and Moor.

Eric frowned, wondering who the FBI mole might be. Devlin would pursue the matter later. He and Cain watched behind a two-way glass window as Devlin, Black and Fox began questioning. Latone looked haggard, Moor worried.

Devlin leaned his hands on the scarred wooden table. "Latone, why did you try to kill Melissa Fagan?"

Latone glanced at his lawyer, then spoke, "I didn't."

"We believe otherwise, Latone. We think you didn't want people to know she was your granddaughter, so you tried to kill her."

"As I explained before, Miss Fagan has no biological relationship to me."

"Hughes admitted that he got your daughter pregnant."

The door opened and Arnold Hughes walked in, a little unsteady with his new leg, but he still had a commanding presence about him. "That's right, but you claimed she lost our baby." Hughes's tone sounded ominous. "Did you give our child away, Robert?"

Latone looked truly nervous for the first time. Moor shifted in his seat, remaining tight-lipped.

"I told you the truth," Latone said. "Candace lost the baby. Melissa Fagan is not your child."

A rap sounded on the door, a uniformed officer came in, handed Devlin a paper, and left. Devlin read it, then stared at Hughes. "His story checks out,

Hughes. Melissa Fagan is not your daughter. She's also not Candace Latone's child.''

Eric gripped the window edge in shock. If Candace Latone wasn't Melissa's mother, who had given birth to her?

Hughes sank into one of the hardback chairs. "So, she's really not my daughter? I thought after all these years…maybe…''

Latone fisted his hands on the table. "Did you kill Candace, Arnold?''

Hughes shook his head. "No, why would I?''

Latone spun toward Moor, accusation in his eyes. "It was you, wasn't it?'' His face turned ashen. "You killed my daughter.''

Moor glared at Latone. "I was trying to protect you, Robert. Candace was nothing but a sick tramp, a black hole of need, and a detriment to you all these years.''

"I loved my daughter,'' Latone said, his temper rising. "She was not a danger to me.''

"What if she had spilled the truth?'' Moor stood and paced, furious. "I was trying to protect you. When that Fagan woman came asking questions, I was afraid Candace would expose the truth. Then your reputation, your career, everything we've worked for all these years would be ruined.''

Latone vaulted across the table and attacked Moor, trying to choke him. Black and Fox dragged them apart and thrust them back into the chairs.

"So, you killed Candace?'' Devlin said to Moor.

Moor nodded, rubbing his neck. "For him.''

"I never asked you to kill my own daughter.''

"No, but you did ask me to assume responsibility

for keeping your reputation intact, and just as always, you left the dirty details up to me.'' He shrugged. ''This time was no different.''

Devlin interrupted before the situation became more volatile. ''Latone, you dropped Melissa off at the church, didn't you?''

Latone nodded.

''So, if Melissa Fagan wasn't Candace's child, who were her parents, and why did you abandon her at the church?'' Black asked.

Latone's lawyer shot him a warning look, but Latone seemed to realize all was lost. He wiped sweat from his forehead. ''The night Candace's baby died, she was so distraught. She…wasn't herself, she had an emotional imbalance, all because she had a reaction to those experimental birth control pills. The pills caused the baby to have birth defects.''

''The reason I spearheaded research to improve intelligence in infants,'' Hughes said.

To create the perfect child. Project Simon. Eric grimaced and glanced at Cain.

''But Candace was beyond reason. She was so upset, she was out of her mind,'' Latone said. ''In the middle of the night, she kidnapped a newborn from the nursery.''

''Melissa Fagan?'' Devlin asked.

Latone nodded, looking miserable. ''When I found out, I figured if the police discovered what she'd done, they'd arrest her and lock her up for life.''

''So, you took the baby to a church and abandoned her instead of returning her to her parents?''

''What else could I have done?'' Latone bellowed.

"If I'd carried her back to the hospital, I would have had to explain. Candace was *my* baby, I felt responsible, I had to protect her."

Eric's heart pounded. He wanted to tear the man apart limb by limb. He had essentially destroyed Melissa's life to protect his sick daughter and his own reputation.

"But Candace never forgave me. She got it in her head that Melissa was really hers, and she...she was never the same."

The room grew quiet as the revelations registered.

Finally, Devlin directed his comments to Moor, "So, you arranged with Dr. Hopkins to brainwash a hired man to kill Candace, then Melissa?"

Moor nodded and glanced at Latone, but Latone gave him a bitter unforgiving look.

Eric's jaw tightened. The pieces had all come together. Latone, Moor, Hughes, Hopkins—they would all pay for their crimes.

But Melissa had suffered because of all of them. Who were her parents?

Chapter Seventeen

Melissa had spent the longest three days of her life waiting for answers. She wanted closure about Candace's murder and her parents.

But more than that, she wanted Eric.

Would he ever change his mind and see her? Could he forgive her for her father's crimes against him? Or would she always remind him of Hughes and the explosion?

Maybe he doesn't love you.

If so, she needed to accept the truth and move on. Maybe return to Atlanta. Although she enjoyed her work at CIRP, she didn't belong here, not after all the bad memories....

She poured herself a cup of coffee, brushed through her hair, preparing to go to work, when a knock sounded. Hope that it might be Eric flickered through her.

She hurried and answered the door, a smile of relief coming when she actually saw him on her doorstep. He still looked serious, haunted, a little leaner from his surgery, but so handsome that her heart swelled with love.

"Can I come in, Melissa? We have to talk."

"Yes." Talk would be good, at least a start.

He followed her to the living area, his limp pronounced.

"You need to continue therapy."

"I will." He waited until she sat on the sofa, then claimed the chair opposite her. "I have some news about the case."

Nerves fluttered in her stomach. "You found out who killed Candace?"

"Yes." Eric leaned his elbows on his knees. "Edward Moor, Robert Latone's assistant. Apparently, he thought he was protecting Latone from his own daughter."

"Did Robert Latone know what Mr. Moor had done?"

Eric shook his head no. "But Latone wanted the two of us out of the picture."

"We were getting too close to the truth?"

"Exactly." Eric sighed. "Hughes was working with Dr. Hopkins on brainwashing experiments, so Moor contacted him, and Hopkins hypnotized this thug to be his hired gun."

"So they would have an alibi?"

"Exactly. Meanwhile, Hughes assumed the identity of an old war buddy. If we'd checked the patient files, we might have made the connection earlier. But there's more." Eric glanced up into her eyes for the first time. "Latone wanted to protect Candace, so he gave you away, but Candace Latone is not your mother."

Melissa gasped. "What?"

Eric gave her a somber look. "Apparently, Candace lost her own baby in childbirth. The baby had birth defects due to the experimental drugs Hughes had given her. Candace was so distraught and inconsolable that she kidnapped a newborn from the nursery."

"The newborn…" Her voice faded. "It was me?"

Eric nodded. "When Latone discovered the kidnapping, he didn't want the police to arrest Candace, so he carried you to the church and left you."

Melissa rubbed her forehead, seeing the events and the way they'd played out. "Instead of returning me to my real parents."

"Yes."

So selfish. So many people hurt, lives changed. "And my real parents, then, who are they?"

"Your mother is waiting outside."

"What?"

"I found her for you, Melissa. It's a present to make up for—"

"You don't have anything to make up for, Eric."

"Then call it my goodbye gift." He stood then, bent and kissed her lips, and limped to the door. She sat in stunned silence as he walked out, struggling to comprehend all that had happened.

Who was her mother? Louise? The woman who'd been so confused…

A second later, Helen, the nurse she'd been working with at the hospital, appeared in the doorway. She looked hesitant, shaken, emotional.

Melissa stared at her in shock. "Helen?"

Helen's eyes filled with tears. "Melissa…I…I can't

believe this, but Mr. Caldwell, he found proof. You're…I'm…you're my baby.''

"How?" Melissa's throat closed. "Are you sure?"

"I thought…you were kidnapped, but…I was told you were a boy. I've looked for you for all these years, but I've been searching for a son."

"A son?"

"Yes." Helen swiped at her eyes. "When you mentioned you were looking for your parents, it never occurred to me that you could be my child."

"And that's the reason you acted so oddly when I asked about the labor and delivery wing."

"I couldn't talk about it," Helen admitted. "It was just too hard. I…wanted a baby so badly." She hugged her stomach. "The night they told me you'd been kidnapped, I wanted to die."

Melissa pressed her hand to her mouth. "My father?"

Tears flowed down Helen's cheeks. "He died before you were born. I had to go on alone, and there were times…times I didn't think I'd survive."

Melissa took a step forward. "I know…I felt the same way." But she had to be sure, she'd thought Candace was her mother. "Wait here just a minute." She ran to the bedroom and retrieved the tiny crocheted bonnet from the keepsake box, then returned with it pressed lovingly in her hands.

"Oh, my heavens." Helen's face paled as she spotted the cap. "You kept it…I made that with my own hands…."

Melissa enveloped Helen into a hug and sagged

against her, both dissolving into tears of joy. Neither one of them would ever have to be alone again.

After all these years and nearly getting killed, she had finally come home.

There was only one thing missing…Eric.

THREE WEEKS LATER, Eric sat on the boat dock behind his cabin on Lake Lanier, the slow lull of the water against the embankment soothing his agitated mind. He had spent the past few weeks recovering and trying to put the past behind him.

But he couldn't forget Melissa.

Sweet, strong, gutsy Melissa who had challenged him to walk, who had kissed his scars and confessed that she loved him, who had given him her virginity and hope when he thought he had none left for his life.

Every whisper of the wind brought memories of her strength and courage. Every night he lay awake, imagining her in his arms. Wishing he'd been good enough for her, courageous enough to be the kind of man to fulfill her dreams.

At least she had her mother now—the family she had always wanted.

And he had Cain and Alanna and Simon.

So why did he still feel lonely?

A car engine purred in the distance, and he pivoted, fishing line in hand. Cain and Alanna had been checking on him regularly. Devlin had even offered him a job, but Eric had declined, the ranch idea growing in his mind.

A familiar Camry pulled into his driveway, and he tensed. Melissa?

Was something wrong?

He held his breath as she exited the car and glanced around. Then she spotted him on the dock and strode toward him. His hands tightened around the fishing pole.

"Eric?"

She looked more beautiful now, rested, a soft pink rosiness to her cheeks that hadn't been there before. And she was smiling. Tentative, but a real smile. God, she looked gorgeous in that slinky sundress with her long hair spilling across her shoulders and the wind kissing her cheeks. He wanted to kiss her....

"Melissa, what are you doing here?"

"I had to see you."

"Is something wrong?"

"Yes."

"Your mother? Did things not work out?"

"No, Helen is fine." Melissa smiled. "Thank you for finding her, she's the family I never had."

"I'm glad. I want you to be happy."

"I am. Except there's still something missing."

His heart pounded, and he started to stand, but she dropped to the dock beside him, letting her feet dangle over the edge of the water. "I have to ask you something."

"What?" Anything. He'd do anything for her.

"Do you blame me for the things Hughes did?"

He grunted in shock. "Of course not. Why would I?"

She shrugged. "Is there someone else?"

"Excuse me?"

"Another woman?" She gestured toward the cabin. "Here, in Atlanta, is there another girl in your life?"

He was so starved for her, he studied her face, memorized her eyes. "No, there's no one else." Didn't she know there never had been?

She bit down on her bottom lip, then turned toward him, her eyes full of emotion. "Then why can't you love me?"

A raspy breath escaped him. She had been so honest with him, so giving, had helped him through so much. Cain said he was a fool for not pursuing a relationship with her.

"Is it because you want to be single? Do you like your single life?"

"Uh, no." He hated it. The empty bed. The TV dinners. The quiet. Whereas once the lake felt peaceful, now it felt lonely.

She pressed her hand over her heart. "Then is something wrong with me?"

"How can you ask that?" He couldn't resist. She looked so vulnerable, soft, delicious. "You're the most perfect woman I've ever known, Melissa."

She wet her lips. "Then why? Is it because of my seizures?"

"No. Hell no." He cleared his throat, studied his fingernails. "You deserve someone better than me, someone stronger, whole." Anger churned through him, and he stood, hating that his leg still hadn't completely healed, and he had to grab the post to support himself. "I'm broken down."

She stood, her voice husky. "Eric, you are the most

stubborn man I've ever met. But I love you, and I want you.'' Tears laced her voice. ''Don't make me beg.''

He clutched her arms, aching to drag her to him. ''You don't have to beg.''

''Do you love me? Yes or no?'' She stared him straight in the eyes. ''Say no, on your mother's cross, and I'll walk away and never bother you again.''

She would always bother him, haunting his memories with her tenderness and strength. His chest squeezed, his throat closed. He glanced down at the cross that had become a symbol for so much in his life. For his mother's dreams, his own hopes.

He couldn't lie.

And he didn't want Melissa to walk away and never come back. He wanted her to stay, to kiss his scars, to hold him all through the night. And he wanted to do the same for her. ''I...''

''Yes or no, Eric?''

He closed his eyes. He wanted her as his wife. ''Yes.''

''Yes, what?'' she whispered.

''Yes, I love you.'' The admission liberated him, opened up the dark vortex in his soul and filled it with sunshine. He opened his eyes, and caught her smiling.

Once he'd said the words, they kept spilling out. ''I love you, Melissa, I love you with all my heart.''

She laughed, and he clinched his arms around her waist and spun her around, a giddy feeling bursting inside him. Then he raised his head and shouted it to the wind and the sky. ''I love Melissa Fagan. I love you, love you, love you!''

Melissa looped her arms around his neck, cradled

his face in her hands and pressed her mouth to his. "So, show me, lover boy."

And he did.

He spread a blanket on the grass beneath a shady oak, stripped her clothes and made slow, sweet love to her until the sun faded into the night, and she promised to be his wife.

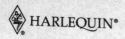

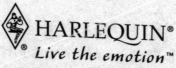

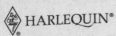

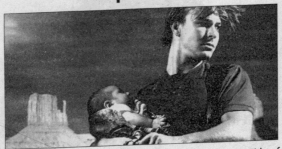
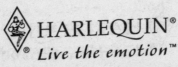

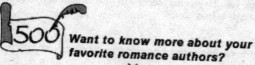

JASMINE CRESSWELL

Art gallery owner Melody Beecham was raised in the elite
social circles of her English mother, Rosalind, and her American
father, Wallis Beecham, a self-made millionaire. But when
her mother dies suddenly, a shocking truth is revealed:
Wallis is not Melody's father. Worse, he is a dangerous man.

And now a covert government agency known as Unit One
has decided to recruit Melody, believing her connections
will be invaluable in penetrating the highest political
circles. They will stop at almost nothing to have
Melody become one of them....

DECOY

"Cresswell skillfully...portrays characters who will interest
and involve the reader."
—*Publishers Weekly* on *The Conspiracy*

*Available the first week of
February 2004 wherever
paperbacks are sold!*

MIRA®

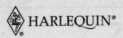

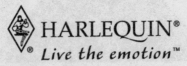